A Cup of Autumn

A Cup of Autumn

A Silver Falls Romance

Melissa McClone

TULE
PUBLISHING

Dedication

To Deb Bishko, Elana Johnson, Melanie Snitker, Julie Trettel and Terri Reed. Thanks for your friendship and always being there to check in with me exactly when I need it the most. Love you lots!

Special thanks to Debbie Bishko and Tara Lampert for answering my research questions. Anything I got wrong is completely my fault.

Chapter One

O N MOST DAYS, customers filling every seat at Tea Leaves and Coffee Beans thrilled Raine Hanover. Today, the eighth of September, wasn't one of those days. She leaned her head to the right and then to the left, trying to relieve the tension in her neck, spine, and shoulders.

The stretching didn't help. Her muscles tightened more.

Not surprising.

She'd been running nonstop since she unlocked the doors at twenty-three minutes after six.

Twenty-three minutes late.

Raine blew out a breath. That was better than releasing a long, drawn-out sigh and filling her coffee shop with way too much carbon dioxide.

Keep going.

She was trying. Okay, maybe not as hard as she should, but today *was* supposed to be her day off. The same as Saturday. And the Wednesday before that.

But nope.

Raine had worked thirteen days in a row. Not that she was counting.

She placed a hazelnut latte on the counter. "Beth."

Okay, Raine was totally counting.

She returned to the espresso machine to prepare the next order—a double espresso for Mrs. Jones, who must be taking the drink to her husband, who owned the hardware store. Mrs. Jones's favorite beverage was a chai latte, and she came in twice a week for them, sometimes three times.

Focus.

Raine couldn't afford to let customer service and satisfaction slip. Making sure Tea Leaves and Coffee Beans remained profitable was her top priority.

But she was tired.

Bone-weary, caffeine-no-longer-helped, running-on-fumes tired.

Close-to-giving-up tired?

Nope, and she wouldn't allow herself to get that way.

The coffee shop was her lifeline—her everything.

No pets, plants, parents, or partner.

Only this place.

It was more than enough.

Suck it up.

That was what she needed to do.

Small business owners worked long hours. She was used to that. The difference this time was the staffing issues. They were the worst they'd ever been. But unfortunately, she was stuck.

If Raine could get rid of Heather, a part-time employee who was supposed to open this morning, she would. She'd dreamed about letting Heather go most nights for the past two weeks. Nightmares, however, fluctuated with pleasant dreams, leaving Raine even more tired. Her subconscious must be working overtime.

Unlike Heather.

But Raine couldn't fire the woman.

At least not when she was down two employees and had been for months. Now that Emmett was out of her life and her heart for good this time, she no longer had a backup—her person—to count on. Maybe not having someone to rely upon made her current situation appear worse, but even if Emmett was around, she would still need extra help.

On the twenty-second of August, Timmy, who'd worked there from day one, had started classes at Summit Ridge University, located in the next town over from Silver Falls, so his availability had lessened, more than either of them expected. She missed seeing what color his hair was each week—sometimes day.

Who was she kidding?

What she really missed was his eagerness to work any shift he could, but school came first. They both agreed upon that. He'd worked too hard during his years attending community college part-time so he could transfer and finish his degree full-time at the university. Even if his absence left her in a world of hurt and needing to hire two or three more baristas. But finding people who wanted to work was proving to be…difficult.

Beth Owen, the owner of the Falls Café a block away, picked up her drink. She peered over the counter. "Just you today?"

"Heather called out." Raine prided herself on not adding

again. She brushed a stray strand of hair from her face with her forearm. Chopping off her hair in a moment of weakness had been a bad idea—too short for a ponytail now. "Sorry, it took so long."

"Don't apologize." Beth took a sip. "Good help is hard to find."

"Try impossible." Raine hadn't yet sipped any coffee, which must be lukewarm in her cup by now. Granted, she could refill it. But the availability wasn't the issue. Time was. And she wasn't in the best mood without a cup first thing in the morning. "I thought hiring staff when I first opened would be hard. Four years later, I wish I could go back to that time when I turned applicants away. Too bad I can't clone Timmy…"

Beth nodded with a gaze full of understanding. "Silver Falls has grown so much. The community's great, but let's not kid ourselves. No state income tax in Washington is one of the draws, and many want to escape bigger cities. But with new businesses opening here and in Summit Ridge, people have more choices for jobs."

"I should be happy for the economic boom, but it's—"

"Hard on employers."

So hard. "I spoke to Mr. Bell, the career counselor at the high school, about hiring a few students for weekend shifts, but I also need others here during the week. I placed an ad on Summit Ridge University's job website. Students would have to commute, so I upped the pay."

"The price of desperation. When we needed a new dishwasher, it took us weeks, but we finally hired someone, and it was for more than we paid the last person. You'll find someone."

Raine crossed her fingers behind her back. If an applicant was breathing and showed up on time, they had a job.

Yep, desperate.

"I take it you won't be attending the First Avenue Business Association meeting that starts..." Beth glanced at her phone "...in five minutes."

"Unfortunately, no." Raine would be more worried if she hadn't coordinated the Valentine event earlier this year.

"Do you need me to take anything over for you?" Beth asked.

Anything meant the nectar of First Avenue aka Raine's special "Silver Falls" coffee blend. She concocted that in honor of the town. "Callie picked up the carafes ten minutes ago."

"Good."

The relief in Beth's voice brought a much-needed smile to Raine's face. She loved pleasing customers and friends. Beth counted as both.

"We were disappointed when you missed last month." Beth raised her cup. "That's why I stopped by for this. In case it happened again."

Raine hadn't had time to deliver coffee to the meeting last month. This morning, she'd called Callie on her way to work. "I plan on attending next month."

If the stars and moon aligned.

She hoped they did.

The association would discuss the annual Holiday Window Decorating Contest at the October meeting. The Christmas windows brought tourists to town and publicity to the storefronts along First Avenue. The definition of a big deal. But the association kept making new rules and coming up with ridiculous fines for businesses, which annoyed her and other business owners. The increase in revenue was nice, but the pressure from the events made Raine question her membership. She wanted to be there to speak up if new regulations were to be voted upon. Few went against Margot Winslow and the other long-time association members, but the last round of fines issued during July's Summer Fair had been too much.

She smiled at Beth. "Hope the meeting goes well."

"See you around." Beth headed toward the exit.

Raine finished preparing the drink and set it on the counter. "Mrs. Jones."

Raine peered into the display case to fill the next order. She grabbed a blueberry muffin—the last one—and placed it on a plate.

Inventory was low.

Her stomach clenched.

Typical for this time of day, but she had no one to send across the street to Lawson's Bakery for refills. Taryn, the owner, would be at the meeting, and her staff wouldn't have time to deliver if Raine called in an order.

Customers would have to order something else or walk across the street to Lawson's.

It is what it is had become Raine's catchphrase.

Be careful what you wish for was a close second.

She poured a cup of French roast and set it next to the muffin. "Mr. Hurley."

She wiped her hands on the front of her apron and made a cappuccino. As her fingers touched a knob on the espresso machine, she let them linger.

Love this place.

Despite the staffing issues, Raine loved the business she'd created, pouring her heart, soul, and inheritance into Tea Leaves and Coffee Beans after working half her life for every type of coffee shop imaginable, from big franchises to mom-and-pop shops. She'd left Seattle and moved to Silver Falls to make her dream come true.

When she met the man she thought she'd marry, her future had been so clear in her mind. It was a good one. She'd not only gotten a boyfriend but also found a new family with his. Until Emmett, who'd grown up in Silver Falls, decided small-town life wasn't for him in January. They'd dated long distance. Broke up in February. Tried a long-distance relationship again. Then in April, he'd decided Raine wasn't for him either. They'd broken up for good that time.

Still worth it.

Even on days like today when things didn't go as well as she'd hoped, Raine kept telling herself that.

Worth it.

All she had to do was keep going.

She *would* find more reliable employees like Timmy. The shop would continue to thrive. She just knew it.

The only question was…how long would that take?

FORGET DEAD WEEK. The Scandinavian Studies department had never been this quiet in the lead-up to finals. Assistant Professor Keaton Andrews even left the door to his office open when it wasn't office hours. Might as well enjoy the peace until the students arrived in a couple of weeks.

Living on the edge.

He grinned, even though the only edge in his life was on his desk where he sat. Sometimes pens fell off when he wasn't paying attention to his surroundings, which wasn't often. Callie, his younger sister, called him the brainy professor. That was better than an absent-minded one.

The syllabus for Introduction to Norwegian Folklore filled his computer screen.

The class always received stellar reviews, but he'd spent the summer revamping the content. He wanted students to fall in love with the subject the way he had as a college freshman. That meant ensuring the lessons ignited a fire inside the young women and men who'd registered for the class. Which was why he was working so hard to make the curriculum as close to perfect as he could.

He laughed.

Overachievers R Us.

A family trait except for the baby of the family, Callie, who'd followed her heart, and she was by far the happiest of them all. Though Garrett had slowed down, too, and had no complaints.

Keaton might want to rethink his goal. Trying to capture his entire class roster was *slightly* ambitious. A more reasonable goal should be one.

If one student discovered a new passion, Keaton would be satisfied. Now to make the class better. He had time to reach perfection or close to it.

Colleges with semesters were in session. Keaton's university followed the quarter system. That meant courses didn't begin until September 26th, less than three weeks from now.

He had a feeling the entire fall quarter would drag.

Who was he kidding?

Keaton wanted classes to be over with before they even began. Don't get him wrong. He loved teaching, but after being on tenure track at an elite university in Los Angeles, his dream of becoming a full-fledged professor was about to come true. He'd submitted his dossier months ago. Now all he had to do was wait until the end of fall quarter for the official tenure announcement to be made.

Professor Keaton Andrews.

He tapped the tips of his leather shoes against the carpet under his desk. His body, however, remained ramrod straight. His posture as perfect as ever.

Anyone glancing into his office would assume he was hard at work, the quintessential professional—the way he'd acted since he stepped foot onto campus to fulfill his dream six years ago.

Nothing, however, would speed up the approval process, so he'd better get back to work.

Keaton focused on the timeline. It still wasn't right.

The phone on his desk rang.

He startled, nearly knocking over his water bottle. No one outside the university used the landline number. He picked up the receiver. "Keaton Andrews, Scandinavian Studies."

"Hi," a friendly female voice greeted him. "It's Lilia. Dean Fredricks would like to see you."

"When?"

"Now."

That was…unexpected. But one didn't keep a dean waiting. Keaton had learned that his second day there.

He jumped to his feet. "On my way."

Keaton saved his file, straightened his bow tie, adjusted his suspenders, and ran his fingers through his hair. He considered putting on his jacket, but the building was warm enough with the temperatures in the low eighties. As much as students paid in tuition, one would think working air conditioners would be in every building. That wasn't the case.

Three minutes later, he approached the dean's assistant's desk. "Should I go in?"

Lilia motioned to the office behind her. The door was ajar. "He's waiting for you. When you're finished, I want to see photos of Rex."

"My sister sent me new ones."

Thinking about Callie's Lab mix brought back memories of the weeks Keaton had spent in Silver Falls, Washington, this summer. He'd attended Callie and Brandt's wedding in July and stayed through mid-August to dog-sit his canine nephew while the newlyweds honeymooned.

He planned to return during winter break for the holidays. Nothing like a white Christmas in a quaint small town where everyone knew his name.

"Rex gets cuter every day." Not that Keaton was biased. The dog was the best. "I'm his favorite uncle. Not even Garrett will replace me."

Garrett, his middle brother, lived in Silver Falls now.

Lilia tsked. "Sounds like you need your own dog."

Callie had mentioned the same thing. Her aunt-in-law Margot, however, hinted Keaton needed a girlfriend.

Both were wrong.

Keaton dated occasionally. But his focus was his career. At least until the official tenure announcement came out. "Maybe for Christmas."

A way to celebrate the holidays and tenure.

Njord or *Magni* might be a good name for a Norwegian Elkhound. Forget one of those tiny, ankle-biter types. He wanted a dog who could keep up with him during walks and hikes.

"You know." A mischievous expression formed on Lilia's face. "Halloween's next month. You could get a dog costume and pass out candy with him or her in a doggy costume to the trick-or-treaters."

A pet came after tenure. He wasn't changing his plans. But Lilia didn't need to know that. "Kids don't come to my apartment building so I stopped buying candy."

"That's an excuse. Two months before Christmas wouldn't make a difference."

Except Keaton had planned everything out. He didn't mess with those plans whether they were written down or in his head. Change wasn't a four-letter word, but it might as well be. Adaptability wasn't a strength, and why academia suited his personality perfectly. "Better not keep the big man waiting."

With a wide smile on his face, Keaton entered the elegant office with wood-paneled walls, bookcases, a large walnut desk, framed Ivy League diplomas on the walls, and large windows with a view of the quad below.

Someday, all the best and the brightest minds who attended the university would know Keaton's name when he became a dean.

Goals.

Keaton had them.

Warmth balled in his chest. He couldn't wait for that day to come.

But first tenure and then the rest of his dream would follow.

Dean Fredricks sat behind a massive desk. The lines on his face appeared deeper than usual. He must be training for another marathon. The man enjoyed running with students and did at least two days a week. "Have a seat."

Keaton sat in one of the two leather chairs nearest him. The dean was a man of few words unless standing behind a podium in a lecture hall, so Keaton remained quiet.

"The university's acceptance rate reached historic lows this past spring." Dean Fredricks adjusted his glasses. "Unfortunately, our yield of attendees was far lower than expected. What happens when tier-one universities fight for the same students. We hoped to fill spots off the waitlist, but we have standards to maintain."

Keaton rubbed his palms over his pants. He didn't know why the dean was telling him this. Unless they'd decided to announce tenure positions early.

He sat taller, placing his hands on his knees so they wouldn't bounce. That had to be the reason, right?

He tried not to smile too widely, given the context of the conversation. Rumors of budget cuts had circulated since spring. The athletic department seemed the likeliest place for cutbacks.

"There's no easy way to say this." The dean's voice dropped an octave. The man brushed his hand through his thinning hair.

A shiver ran along Keaton's spine. That didn't sound like he would be delivering good news. "What?"

"Your department's being cut."

Keaton's jaw dropped. The air whooshed from his lungs. His fingers dug into the chair's leather. The room spun. His vision blurred, and he forced himself to breathe.

"Cut?" The word sounded breathless. The way he felt.

"Some courses will be absorbed into other departments. Others will be canceled." Dean Fredricks stared at his desk. "This must be a shock."

No words. Keaton, who had never been at a loss for what to say, was speechless. He forced himself to nod.

"Tenured professors have been offered the opportunity to move into different departments, but other contracts are canceled, effective immediately."

The hits kept coming. Did Professor Duncan and everyone he'd worked with know? Keaton had seen most this morning when he arrived, and then the department had cleared out. They had to have known what was coming, yet none had warned him. A simple *heads-up* or *heard another rumor* would have prepared him.

Instead, he'd been blindsided.

Keaton's eyelids burned. His chest tightened, the spot where his heart should be aching.

He knew the answer, but his father had taught him to fully understand a situation before jumping to conclusions.

Keaton cleared his throat. "Including mine?"

"Yes."

His stomach roiled. He thought he might throw up.

Keaton had worked so hard. He couldn't walk away without a fight. "I've done everything required of me. For six years. My performance reviews. Publishing more than required. Top course surveys from students."

The dean's gaze finally met Keaton's. "There is no longer a department or a position at this university for you, so tenure is no longer possible. This isn't personal."

Yes, it is. "Working at this university is my life."

My dream. And it was going down in flames.

He forced himself to breathe, but filling his lungs with air took more effort than it should.

"You'll receive recommendations and help in locating a new position." The dean's matter-of-fact tone bristled. "I have no doubt you'll land a choice position by winter."

"Winter?" Keaton stiffened. "Don't I have a year to find another…"

"You only get a terminal year if you're denied tenure."

But he was denied it. Just not officially. "My courses this quarter…"

"Will be taught by someone else."

Most likely Professor Larsen, tenured and overbearing. The students hated the way he droned on about his own family's Norwegian history. And all Keaton's work this summer had been…

For nothing.

His shoulders slumped, but an instant later, he straightened. He needed to remain strong until he was alone.

"The decision to cut your department has been made and is effective immediately," Dean Fredricks continued as if he were talking about using cream-colored copier paper instead of white. "Of course, you'll receive a severance package."

Of course. Keaton nearly laughed. Stuff like this happened to other people, not an Andrews. His family were winners. They didn't lose or fail or get fired. Even Callie had won nine months ago. "Is there an appeal process?"

"No."

He would speak with his father and brother. They were lawyers. Expensive ones in a different field, but they had contacts.

"The less fuss you make the better your chances…elsewhere." The dean's underlying threat brought a chill, bone-deep, followed by goose bumps.

For years, Keaton had looked up to the man. Now, all he wanted to do was get away from him. But he stood his ground, reining in his emotions. No losing control. His livelihood was at stake. "Anything else?"

"HR will speak with you shortly. You should pack up your office."

Keaton's hands balled. He pressed his lips together to keep from saying something he would regret and marched out of the office as if he were setting off to war—outnumbered without a clear strategy on how to win.

He passed Lilia's desk and kept going. He couldn't stop to show her Rex. Not now.

"Keaton," she called out.

Not glancing back—he couldn't—Keaton trudged to his office as if wading through wet cement. He kept going, even though his insides trembled, and the word "failure" echoed in his brain.

His gaze focused on the carpet. As far as he could tell, no one else was in the hallway.

Thank goodness. But that begged a question. More than one.

Which colleagues had been told the news? Offered a new job in another department or school? Fired like him? Who was avoiding him because he was out?

The last question burned the most.

His footsteps echoed.

Keaton undid his bow tie and the top button of his dress shirt. He rolled up his sleeves. Appearances no longer mattered. He'd dressed the part—bought tweed even—and what had it gotten him?

All his hard work had been for nothing.

He stormed into his office and slammed the door behind

him. Framed diplomas rattled against the wall. He didn't care.

The office wasn't much—large enough to hold office hours with a small study group if need be—but it had been his.

Keaton ran his fingertips along the edge of a bookshelf, one of three in the office. The desk, chairs, and bookcases weren't his. But everything that mattered to him was on the shelves and in the drawers.

Books, research, his life.

He rubbed his eyes.

Focus.

Keaton pulled out a phone and typed.

Me: *Met with the dean.*

Me: *My department's been cut.*

Me: *Contract canceled.*

Me: *No tenure and no job.*

Me: *Dad and Garrett, do I have any legal recourse?*

Keaton hit send. The messages would go to their family group chat. Between two lawyers, two doctors, a techie brother-in-law, a baker sister-in-law, and a dog-loving sister, who owned her own business, they would figure this out.

His family had never let him down.

They wouldn't this time.

Chapter Two

A S THE CLOCK struck noon, a whimsical chime sounded. Raine loved the fun clock, a Christmas gift from Callie Andrews, which didn't quite fit the laid-back vibe of the coffee shop, but it was perfect, nonetheless, and from a dear friend, so it hung in a place of honor. Much better there than at Raine's house where she didn't spend as much time.

Raine smiled. She'd survived two more hours on her own.

Go me!

The morning had passed by in a rush, but somehow, she'd filled every order, washed a load of cups, and sipped half a cup of cold coffee.

Caffeine was caffeine no matter the temperature.

Only eight more hours to go until Raine would flip the open sign to closed. Her fingers itched to lock the door now, but she would make it.

What was the phrase Taryn Lawson Andrews used?

Easy-peasy.

That was it.

The shop had cleared out twenty minutes ago, and Raine had raced to the bathroom. Usually, a morning rush meant a lunchtime lull. She would gladly take less business this afternoon.

The bell on the door jingled.

Raine pasted on her best service-with-a-smile expression.

Margot Winslow, in her sixties but a teenager at heart, carried an orange rubber bin with a black lid. She waltzed to the counter dressed in a short-sleeved T-shirt, broomstick skirt, quilted vest with tassels, and Birkenstocks—typical of the quilt-shop owner's boho style.

"Hello." Margot's eyes twinkled like aquamarine gemstones. The closest thing to royalty in Silver Falls, she ruled the First Avenue Business Association like a queen. She set the bin on the counter. "We missed you at the meeting today."

"Sorry about that." Raine readied her finger over the cash register to take the order. "I had no one to cover me."

Margot peered over the counter. "Where's your staff?"

That was the question of the day. "Out."

"You're here alone?"

"Yes." Raine's smile slipped. She forced it back into place. "The usual?"

"Not today." Margot studied the menu board on the wall behind Raine. "I'm overheated from the meeting and need to cool down. I'll have an iced tea. Extra ice with a smidgen of sugar. Oh, please add a lemon slice."

Raine rang up the sale. Margot paid with cash and tucked two dollars into the tip jar.

Usually, Raine left the tips for her staff to split and didn't take a share. Today, the money would be all hers. She would use it to buy dinner after she closed.

Margot remained standing in front of the cash register. That was…odd. Most customers moved to the other end of the counter to pick up their drinks.

Raine filled the stainless shaker with iced tea. "Did you want something else?"

"No. I want to tell you what happened at the meeting."

Margot was also the hub for gossip in town. "Drama?"

"A few tempers spiraled."

That happened when coordinators needed to be assigned to an upcoming event. Sometimes, people were eager to volunteer. Other times not.

Raine added a teaspoon of sugar—what she'd determined Margot considered a smidgen. "What got people so riled?"

"We voted on who would be in charge of the Boo Bash."

"I thought someone was picked in August." Raine shook the mixture.

"No. The Boo Bash coordinator is selected the month before."

Raine had missed that meeting too but assumed…

She filled a plastic cup with ice. "Was it a fight for the position or were there crickets?"

"Crickets."

That meant no one volunteered. The association must have drafted someone. Okay, being selected wasn't as bad as being named a tribute in the Hunger Games, but that might be preferable to juggling the event and a busy real life.

Raine poured the tea into the cup, added a slice of lemon, a lid, and a straw. She set the drink in front of Margot.

"Here you go."

"Thank you." Margot didn't reach for the cup. "I have good news for you."

Raine's heart leapt. She leaned forward. The counter pressed against her stomach. "Do you know someone looking for a job?"

"No, but I'll let you know if I hear of anyone."

She straightened, tamping down her disappointment and picking up the shaker to wash it. "So, what's the good news?"

Margot's smile deepened the laugh lines around her mouth. "We voted for you to be in charge of this year's Boo Bash."

The shaker slipped from Raine's hands. She caught it.

Thank goodness for fast reflexes. Still, her pulse raced as if she'd shot a liter of caffeine straight into her vein. "How? Why? I wasn't there."

"No, but it's your turn."

"No." The word shot out. "I was in charge of the Valentine's Sweetheart Dance in February."

Margot's eyes widened. Her mouth parted as if surprised. "Oh, I forgot. It appears everyone else did too because no one brought that up. But no matter, everyone else is too busy right now to take on the Boo Bash."

Raine's muscles knotted. This was the last thing she needed or could handle. "I've been down an employee for months, and Timmy's cut back his hours because of college. I haven't had a day off in almost two weeks."

"All of us are in a similar position. I'm sorry, but you know the rules. Once voted for, you're it. No take-backs."

Margot patted the bin's lid. "You're the coordinator for this year's Boo Bash. The materials you'll need are inside the box."

Raine opened her mouth and then shut it. Her thoughts were a jumble, but she had to figure out how this happened. "Was the vote unanimous?"

"Callie, Taryn, Pippa, and Beth voted no."

Too bad Anna worked for Callie or that would have been another vote in Raine's favor. At least her friends had stood up for her. That had to count for something. "No take-backs, huh?"

"If you quit, you'll be assessed a significant fine. You know the rules."

"I do, which is why I should have never been nominated in the first place. We're only required to do one event a year. I did that. I organized the Valentine's dance."

Margot said nothing.

Not unexpected. Still, Raine needed to get this out. "I'll be fully transparent and tell you the Boo Bash won't be anything close to what it's been in the past. I don't have the time."

"That's your choice. But you may have fallout from that decision."

"Don't care." Raine didn't. If she had the extra money, she would pay the fine. "This falls on everyone in the association who voted for me when I shouldn't have been up for consideration."

She would make sure the kids had fun trick-or-treating at the shops on their early release day the Wednesday before

Halloween and call it good, but less would be more this year.

Raine had worked hard for the association, including in February after Emmett broke up with her for the first time, and she'd felt empty inside not romantic. She'd given her all then. She had nothing to give now.

Forget about remaining in the association. No way would she renew for next year. Not after they'd done this to her. Now wasn't the time to tell Margot, the founder of the association, who loved it as much as her two dogs and nephew. But enough was enough. A business association should support its members, not enforce rules and assess fines that made their lives harder.

She pushed back her shoulders as if preparing for battle. Given what these events meant to the association and the town, she was in for a fight. "I can handle whatever people have to say. Especially when I remind them how I put on an event earlier this year and should have been exempted from this one."

Harsh, perhaps.

But true.

Just let someone complain, and words would fly. Was it horrible she looked forward to that?

Must be from keeping all the stuff that happened with Emmett inside her for too long.

Surprisingly, Margot's smile spread across her face. "It's good to see you showing some backbone finally."

Raine cringed, even though Margot made a valid point. "Been trying."

And she had.

Ever since July when Emmett showed up unannounced to pick up the boxes he'd left in her garage. His mother wouldn't keep them after he'd moved out of his apartment in January, so he'd dumped them on Raine. He now lived in Seattle, which was where she'd grown up.

They'd swapped hometowns.

Ironic or fitting?

She hadn't decided which.

"You've been through a lot. Emmett's mother said he's enjoying Seattle." Margot's voice was sympathetic. Not unexpected. But she had blinders on when it came to the First Avenue Business Association. "It's time you replaced him."

Like any small town, rumors ran rampant, but this one was one hundred percent true based on the updates to Emmett's social media accounts. Raine still followed him and vice versa. Though seeing him with another woman had stung worse than the hornet she'd come across at the old mill. "It's not only Emmett I need to replace. I need at least two more baristas."

"I'm not talking about work."

Oh.

Oh, no.

A heaviness pressed against Raine's shoulder. This was bad. Not in charge of the Boo Bash bad, but a close second.

Margot fancied herself the town matchmaker. Okay, she'd brought together her nephew, Brandt, and Callie in December. And this summer, she'd managed to get Taryn together with Callie's brother, Garrett.

Whether luck or coincidence, Raine wanted no part of any matchmaking in her life. She wasn't ready to take another shot at love. She might never be ready for that, even if she was over Emmett. The mixture of hurt and disappointment had been too much. It was as if she'd relived losing her parents again. She didn't want to go through that again.

Raine crossed her arms over her chest. "My focus is Tea Leaves and Coffee Beans. With my crazy work hours and the Boo Bash to plan, dating won't be happening for a long time. Please go play matchmaker elsewhere."

"Of course," Margot replied quickly. A little too quickly, which suggested trouble. "Did I imply otherwise?"

"No."

Margot's reputation, however, preceded her. And now, her blue eyes danced. A bad sign that put Raine's sanity at stake, but her relationship status wasn't changing. No matter what Margot had in mind.

Time to shut this down. "Just want to be clear where I stand."

"I hear you." Margot perked up. "And you're in luck."

Yeah, bad luck. Raine's shoulders drooped. "What do you mean?"

"I'm not only a matchmaker. I'm also a headhunter." Margot winked and sipped her iced tea. "No one makes tea blends like you. Now…tell me what you're looking for in a barista?"

Maybe Raine overreacted with her worst-case-scenario-matchmaking thinking. But with two friends saying "I do" recently, she couldn't help herself.

"Reliable with a strong work ethic and breathing. But I don't need a headhunter to find baristas." What Raine needed was a miracle. She hoped her ads did the trick. "I'll figure it out."

"You do that, but I'll keep my ears and eyes open too."

"Thank you." Raine's eyes would be open. She wouldn't be sleeping much with the Boo Bash to organize at night. That was the only time planning the event could happen until she hired more staff. "Enjoy your iced tea."

She placed the Boo Bash's rubber bin behind the counter.

Doable, right?

Raine crossed her fingers again, hoping it would be.

ONLY FOUR DAYS had passed since Keaton had lost his job, but it felt like a lifetime. He paced across the floor of his parents' living room in Beverly Hills. He'd grown up there and knew every inch. If he didn't stop walking, he'd wear a path on the wood floors, but sitting would only make him fidget.

"You must be getting tired." The concern in Mom's voice made him slow down.

"I'm…" Saying okay would be ridiculous. It was a weekday and not his day off. He wore shorts, a T-shirt, and bare feet, not his usual tweed jacket, bow tie, suspenders, dress pants, plaid socks, and leather shoes. His world had turned upside down and inside out. He hated the out-of-control feeling. "I'll sit later."

Everyone was there. Well, those related to him by blood. His new in-laws Brandt Winslow and Taryn Lawson Andrews had stayed in Silver Falls. Rex and Lawson's Bakery most likely the reasons, but Keaton hadn't asked. Not when he was trying to salvage the life he'd so meticulously planned.

Flynn sat on the couch next to Mom. "You'll wear yourself out."

Talk about being a hypocrite. The circles under Flynn's eyes appeared worse than the last time Keaton had seen his oldest brother. "You're one to talk."

Flynn's face hardened. "I'm fine."

Which meant he wasn't. That was almost as shocking as Keaton losing his job. Flynn was the oldest and a renowned surgeon. The playing God part of medicine appealed to him. The guy was as arrogant as he was generous. An odd mix. But Keaton appreciated having Flynn on his side.

"Things at the hospital will slow down soon, and Flynn won't be as tired." Mom, chief of staff where Flynn worked, wrung her hands—something she did when worried. But it wasn't her oldest she was concerned about. Mom barely glanced at Flynn. Her attention had been on Keaton.

He gulped.

For the first time, he was the reason for the hand wringing. The figurative knife in his heart twisted. All he wanted to do was make his family proud and not disappoint them. He'd never imagined he would be the one who failed.

"You're the focus now," Mom added as if he hadn't figured that out himself.

"Welcome to the hot seat, Keaton." Callie had flown in with Garrett as soon as they found out about Keaton losing his job. "Must admit I'm glad it's not me sitting there."

"Or me." Garrett shot Keaton a sympathetic look. "There's a first time for everyone."

It shouldn't be Keaton's. "I was hoping to avoid it."

Dad sat on a wingback chair with his elbows on his thighs and leaning forward slightly. Even with his loosened tie and the rolled-up sleeves of his dress shirt, he would be a formidable opponent in court. "This isn't the end of the world, Son."

"I want to believe that."

Bitterness coated Keaton's mouth like a double dose of cough syrup. He'd had a few days to come to terms with losing his job and his shot at tenure, but he was still reeling. His emotions swung from disbelief to frustration to anger. Everything he'd defined himself as had been stripped away. And one question kept him awake at night.

Who was he without teaching at a prestigious university?

He'd defined himself by his job. He hadn't only lost his income. He'd also lost his identity.

And his purpose in life.

Keaton took a breath and another. "Are you sure there's nothing I can do?"

Dad sat back. "I've consulted with top employment attorneys who specialize in education. The university is within its right to cut your department and cancel your contract."

Keaton shot a glance at Garrett. "Did you find out anything?"

"Sorry, Keaton." After Garrett's plane landed on Friday night, no one saw him until today. He'd been working nonstop to find a way to help Keaton. "Dad's right. There's no recourse to what the university did, but you've got excellent experience, and you're getting solid recommendations."

"Finding a tenure-track position will be difficult." The words flew out of Keaton's mouth as if he were tossing a spear like the Vikings of eons past did. He took a breath. "I thought I was different. That I would beat the odds when I submitted the dossier. I was so sure and now...

"Keaton was born to be a professor," Mom said.

"Thanks, Mom." She worked more hours than Dad and pushed for each of her children to live up to their potential. That drive had annoyed Callie, but Keaton appreciated Mom's support.

"You'll find your place." Callie smiled at him, a bright torch in his pitch-black week. She might be the baby of the family, but she was the glue that held them together. "And in the meantime, I have an idea."

"What is it, sweetheart?" Dad asked in the softer tone he reserved for Mom and Callie.

Callie's face brightened like a ray of sunshine had somehow found its way through the ceiling. She scooted forward in her chair as if to get closer to Keaton. "Come to Silver Falls. You can stay with me and Brandt, or Garrett and Taryn, or Margot if you don't want to be around newlyweds."

Callie and Brandt had had a big wedding. Garrett and

Taryn had eloped in Lake Tahoe, much to the dismay of both sets of parents, who kept asking if they'd have a reception. Both couples were lovey-dovey all the time.

His sister and brother's happiness thrilled Keaton, but a guy could only take so many heart-eyes and so much couple togetherness. "Do you think Margot would mind if I stayed with her?"

"Not at all." Callie didn't hesitate to answer. "She's the one who suggested you come to Silver Falls. She won't charge you rent."

"That's generous of Margot," Mom said.

"She enjoys having house guests." Keaton had stayed at Margot's the week before the wedding. Then, he'd moved to Callie's house when they left on their honeymoon. Margot had invited him over to dinner each Sunday, and he'd taken her out to lunch twice a week. He got the better end of that deal.

"Great idea, baby sis." Garrett rubbed his chin. "Keaton can regroup and apply for jobs."

"And play with Rex." Keaton missed the dog.

Callie rolled her eyes. "Yes, we all know how you bonded with your nephew. Rex would love to see you too."

"I need to move out of my apartment." Rent around the university was expensive, so the school offered subsidized housing to faculty members. They'd given him a month to vacate, but finding a new place made no sense when he was unemployed. "I'll put my stuff in storage."

Until he knew where he would end up.

"Leave your things in my garage. I only use one spot so

you can have the other half. That'll save you a monthly fee."
Flynn yawned.

Keaton's next job might not be in L.A. Few tier-one universities were on the West Coast. To pursue his dream of teaching at one meant he would likely end up on the East Coast. He didn't like the idea of moving away from his parents and oldest brother, but two of his siblings now lived in the same small town in Washington. Their family was changing.

Dad laughed. "He's thinking about it."

Yes, but not about Silver Falls, per se.

"Please come to Silver Falls." Callie's gaze implored Keaton in the same way she used to ask for an extra cookie or for him to play Barbies with her. "I was so busy with the wedding and then you left right after we got home from our honeymoon. I haven't spent time with you beyond Thanksgiving and Christmas."

Garrett side-eyed her. "And both holidays you storm off after we beat you at Monopoly."

Flynn nodded. "Settlers of Catan."

"And cards." There were worse places Keaton could go to regroup. He missed working on his courses in Tea Leaves and Coffee Beans. No one made coffee like Callie's friend Raine. "But you're right. Silver Falls might be a nice change."

Callie jumped to her feet and clapped. "You can relax and research jobs."

"You'll finally have time to finish the novel you started as an undergrad," Mom suggested.

His novel.

Keaton had completed a second draft before pushing aside fiction writing to pursue academic pursuits. Publish or perish wasn't far from the truth for any university's faculty member. Sure, his specialty included folklore, mythology, and legends, but writing about those for papers wasn't the stuff of novels. "I will have the time for it finally."

Time was all he would have. Unfortunately.

He scrubbed his hand over his face.

"The university will regret losing you." Dad's furrowed brow reminded Keaton of when he'd told his dad he didn't want to be a lawyer. Dad had been disappointed, but he never said a negative word and supported Keaton's endeavor to be a professor someday one hundred percent. "Maybe not this week or next month, but a brilliant career lies ahead of you, Son."

"Of course, they'll regret it." Mom didn't miss a beat. "Keaton's irreplaceable."

Keaton shared a glance with his siblings, who all smiled. Their parents were their biggest supporters.

Garrett shook his head, but amusement filled his eyes. "You sound like such a mom right now."

"Well, that's what I am." Mom raised her chin. She turned her attention to Keaton. "When you return to L.A., stay here. Your old room's ready for you."

Keaton appreciated the offer, but he was too old to move home. Unless he had no other place to go. He hoped it wouldn't come to that. "Thanks, but I might stay in Silver Falls for a while."

As soon as he packed up his apartment, moved his stuff into Flynn's garage, got the oil changed in his car, and his tires checked, he would drive north. A free place to stay would keep his expenses low while he applied for jobs. Oh, he'd make sure to help Margot around the house, yard, and in her quilt shop. He'd even cook meals. Anything to repay her kindness.

He wasn't broke, only unemployed. He had a decent severance package and unemployment would kick in if he couldn't find a job. He also had money in savings, but he wanted to be careful with his finances. Finding a tenure-track position would take time.

Keaton hadn't expected to be in Silver Falls until December, but the small town was his best option.

For now, at least.

Chapter Three

ELEVEN O'CLOCK ON the last Monday in September, and the morning rush at the coffee shop hadn't lessened at all. Raine wasn't complaining. Well, not exactly. More customers were good for her bottom line, but this month's increase wasn't due to an additional influx of coffee lovers in Silver Falls. At least, she didn't think so.

Stifling another yawn, Raine added three dots of milk foam to the mocha.

She had three theories to explain the additional traffic at Tea Leaves and Coffee Beans.

Raine squeezed a bottle of chocolate sauce to make circles around each of the foam dots.

The rumor mill was at the top on her list. If town folks heard she was in trouble, they would send business her way. A sweet thought, but the extra traffic was causing her more work with no time for breaks when she was the only one behind the counter.

She used the end of a thermometer to make a circle that cut through each of the foam dots. That left three hearts floating on the top of the mocha.

The second theory involved guilt. Not hers but members

of the First Avenue Business Association. If they realized she shouldn't have been forced to coordinate the Boo Bash, they might bring in more business for her to make up for their mistake. Again, a nice gesture, but it only made working on the upcoming event impossible. Two and a half weeks had passed since Margot dropped off the Boo Bash box, and Raine hadn't had time to open it.

She carefully lifted the drink.

The design wasn't as fancy as others she'd created, but Raine did what she could on her own. Heather had called out yet again. She'd been there for two of seven shifts. Not exactly progress, but Raine hadn't found anyone to hire yet.

Her third theory relied on bad timing, as in the adage "when it rains it pours." Now that fall had arrived, a warm drink appealed to more people.

A fourth option might exist, but she didn't believe in curses. Though if one more interview fell through, she would reconsider their existence.

She placed the cup on the counter. "Taryn."

The next order—a vanilla steamer—wouldn't take long.

Taryn came to the counter in her bakery whites. A net covered her hair. Only her white cap was missing from what the baker wore each day at Lawson's Bakery. Her sparkling diamond engagement ring, the envy of most women and a few men in town, wasn't on her ring finger either. A simple gold wedding band graced her left hand today.

Since eloping with Garrett Andrews, Taryn's face glowed radiantly. But as she peered at her drink, her smile widened. "You made me hearts. Thank you."

"You're a newlywed."

Taryn shimmied her shoulders. "I love being married. Of course, I love my husband too."

A part of Raine envied Taryn and Callie for marrying their Mr. Rights. Both friends deserved happy endings, but Raine had been the one in a committed long-term relationship with Emmett Wilson until January and now... "He loves you so much."

Garrett—the definition of tall, dark, and handsome—wasn't the most attractive of the three Andrews brothers in Raine's opinion. But each man had been blessed with looks, intelligence, and a protective streak for Callie, their younger sister.

Garrett was intense with a capital I. His pointed gaze had once sent a shiver down Raine's spine. That intensity most likely made him a successful defense attorney.

On the flipside, he doted on Taryn and Callie. He'd shown such concern when Brecken, the bakery's then-youngest employee, disappeared in July, and asked his two brothers to find the teen so he could stay with Taryn, which they all, Raine included, appreciated.

She wasn't looking for someone like Garrett. Or Callie's Brandt for that matter.

What did a barista have in common with men whose jobs required college degrees and super-duper brain power?

Not much when picking what TV show to binge or what to fix for dinner required too much thinking for her.

Someday, Raine hoped to find a guy who not only loved her but also wanted the same things out of life that she did in the same place as her. If he had a couple tattoos and piercings like Emmett, even better. She'd never colored inside the lines. Why start now?

"Any luck hiring a new barista?" Taryn asked.

The question jolted Raine. "I've set up eight interviews. All the applicants ghosted me. I don't get it."

"I'm sorry. I hope you find the right employees soon. You can't keep up this pace."

Last night, Raine had fallen asleep on the couch. Thank goodness she'd set her alarm ahead of time, or she might have arrived late this morning. "I don't have a choice."

"I understand." Taryn's chin lifted. "When I lost half my staff to the bakery in Summit Ridge, I don't know what I would have done if Jayden, Carl, and Brecken had left too."

"Their loyalty paid off. Now, Brecken's sister works for you."

"I'm so lucky to have Mandy. And you will be too when you hire more people."

"Brecken has other siblings, right? Think I can hire one of them?"

"Unfortunately, the next oldest is only thirteen. You'll have to wait a couple of years."

Raine laughed. "Waiting has been the story of my life."

Waiting for Emmett to make up his mind about a long-distance relationship. Waiting to find out if they would survive as a couple living hours away from each other. Waiting for the right employees to cross her path.

Raine was tired of it.

Taryn picked up her drink. She added a lid to the cup. "I

must get back to the bakery. It's bread baking time."

As Raine worked on the steamer, the scent from the sweet vanilla mixture made her mouth water. The consequence of skipping breakfast.

She added frothed milk to the top. Two dollops of whipped cream went on next. She set the cup on the counter. "Savannah."

Eight-year-old Savannah Baxter skipped toward the counter without a care in the world. The slumped shoulders of her mother, Robin, told another story.

The woman's designer clothes hadn't changed, but the mother of two no longer wore perfectly applied makeup. Her pale complexion, sunken eyes, and messy bun spoke volumes about her soon-to-be ex-husband's money and legal problems and the for-sale sign hanging in the front yard of their mansion.

"I fell at recess. Cut myself. There was so much blood. Got stitches." Savannah raised her chin to show them off. "Mommy said I got a treat on the way back to school."

"You were brave." Robin touched her daughter's thin shoulder. "You deserve something special."

Savannah picked up the cup and sipped. "Yummy."

"I hope you heal quickly." A few weeks, maybe a month, had passed since either had come into the shop or been out and about in town. "I hope the steamer helps you feel better."

Raine didn't believe in guilt by association. Robin was a friend, who'd been married to a jerk. Okay, she'd stood by Nick when he'd shown his true colors nearly seven years ago with his treatment of his so-called best friend Brandt Winslow. But after Nick tried to ruin Lawson's Bakery and Callie and Brandt's wedding, Robin had filed for divorce in July.

Raine had silently applauded the stay-at-home mom of two. She poured Robin a cup of the house blend, added a teaspoon of sugar, and a dash of cream, and placed it on the counter. "This coffee's for you, Robin."

Robin jolted to a stop. Her lips parted but no words came out. The whites of her eyes, however, reddened.

She picked up the coffee and sipped. An almost rapturous expression formed on her face. "Th-thanks."

The two walked away.

"Robin." The name sprung from Raine's lips like the spring runoff over Silver Falls. Something had compelled her to call out, but she didn't know what. Robin stopped and turned. "Yes?"

The uncertainty in the one word nearly broke Raine's heart. She hated to think how Robin might have been treated by Nick over the years...or lately. "If you hear of anyone looking for a job, could you please tell them I'm hiring?"

Something flashed in Robin's eyes.

Dare it be interest?

"I might know someone." Robin wet her lips. "What kind of experience are you looking for?"

"The ability to learn, a desire for hours, and patience would come in handy during the busy times, but that's not a requirement."

Robin half laughed. "Setting the bar high, huh?"

"You have no idea."

Robin glanced at Savannah who wore a milk-foam mustache. "Thanks for telling me about the position. I'll keep it in mind."

For herself or someone else?

Didn't matter. Raine had put the offer out there. That was all she could do.

Time to fill the next order. She glanced at the list.

Huh? Raine peered closer. Inhaled sharply.

Not one order remained.

All caught up! Finally.

She pumped her fist.

This was cause for celebration or to escape into the office to peek inside the Halloween bin.

The bell on the front door jingled.

Or maybe not.

Raine wiped her hands and stood behind the cash register with a cheerful smile. She glanced at the person approaching the counter and did a double take.

She hadn't expected to see Callie's brother Keaton walking toward her with a worn-leather laptop bag, something he'd carried with him each time he came into the coffee shop.

Raine had met him last Christmas. He'd returned to Silver Falls for six weeks this summer. Callie wasn't a fan of her brother's smarter-than-you attitude, but Keaton tipped well, didn't say much while he worked, and provided some nice eye candy while Raine worked.

"What are you doing in Silver Falls?" she asked.

"Visiting family." He strode to the counter with a grace more fitting of an athlete than an academic. He was taller than his brothers and thinner. His thick plastic glasses gave him a nerdy vibe. Nerdy, but geeky cute. Probably why Callie's nickname for him was the brainy professor.

He was the most attractive of the three Andrews brothers, but the antithesis of Raine's usual type. She had a thing for biker bad boys. Even if her exes only dressed the part, something about that look drew her in.

Today, Keaton's Henley and faded jeans made him look younger, more approachable than when he wore a bow tie, dress shirt, tweed pants, and suspenders. She liked the casual style on him.

As her muscles relaxed, her smile came naturally. "I didn't think you were coming back until Christmas."

His attention jerked to hers. He may have even shrugged. "Change of plans."

Surprising. He seemed more like a person whose plans had plans than an impromptu type. At least based on what Callie had mentioned.

Keaton stared at the menu.

Another surprise. "You're not ordering an Americano?"

He'd ordered those during every visit, even when Callie wanted to order Christmas cocoas for her family in December.

"Seeing what's new," he said.

"Fall's here, so I added pumpkin spice drinks to the menu."

"Guess you can't avoid that this time of year."

"Nope. It's a cup of autumn. People love it." Raine thought the flavor was overrated, but her customers drank it up, so she created more for them to order. "Anything call to your taste buds?"

"Something with pumpkin spice," he said finally. "Surprise me."

O-kay. That was strange, but he was the customer. She wrote his name on a cup. "Callie was in yesterday. She didn't mention you were in town."

"I arrived last night. I'm staying with Margot. Figured that would be better than staying with—"

"Newlyweds."

"Exactly."

Raine remembered conversations. That was how she knew what customers drank. She set the machine.

Something about his visit felt off. It wasn't his casual clothes or letting her pick his drink. And then she remembered.

"You're on the quarter system, right?" She wished Summit Ridge University wasn't on semesters or Timmy would be working his usual shifts.

"You're correct." He might not look like a professor, but he sounded like one. "Classes begin today. I'm not teaching this quarter."

Weird. She remembered him excited about revamping the curriculum. He'd been so enthusiastic and mentioned a few foreign words. One had sounded like a superhero character. "Taking time off for research?"

His expression froze. It thawed two seconds later, but his

eyes had dimmed. "Something like that."

Raine rang up the drink.

He paid with cash and tucked a dollar into the tip jar. "Thanks."

"Be glad you came in when you did, or you'd be waiting for a bit."

"Been crowded?"

She placed a cup under the nozzle and adjusted the knobs. "It was, and I'm on my own."

He glanced around. "Where's Timmy?"

"College. Full-time this semester. He's only working weekends and two evenings a week now."

"Good for him."

Raine nodded. "It is, but I need to find weekday replacements."

The coffee shop's phone rang. She glanced toward the office where she must have left the receiver when she spoke to a supplier.

"Go answer it." Keaton motioned for her to go. "I don't mind waiting."

"Thanks." She hurried and answered the phone. "Tea Leaves and Coffee Beans. This is Raine."

"It's Margot."

"What can I get for you?" Raine didn't want to be curt, but she didn't want to make Keaton wait too long.

"Two cappuccinos, one hot chocolate, a mocha, and a pumpkin spice latte. It's for my quilt workshop. My coffee isn't as good as yours."

Raine stood taller. "Thanks. I'll prepare your order, but

I'm short-staffed again, so I can't deliver."

"No worries." Margot sounded as if she were brushing away a gnat. "I'll send someone over. We haven't been busy this morning."

"I wish I could say the same."

"Be careful what you wish for. Bye." Margot disconnected from the call.

Raine held on to the phone. She would put it underneath the counter where she could answer it more easily. She turned.

Keaton stood behind the counter and refilled a cup.

With a smile, he handed the cup to a customer, who wasn't a regular. "Have a nice day."

She walked toward him. "Bored?"

"Figured I'd lend a hand. I saw your daily blends on the back counter."

"Thank you. But be careful. I need to hire people. You're so good at this I'm tempted to hand you an apron, and put you to work."

"Yeah, right," he joked.

"Good help is impossible to find. An employee who is proactive like you would be a dream come true."

His chest puffed. "I would be, but can you see me as a barista?"

Yes, she wanted to shout.

"Don't you think I'm overqualified for the job?" he asked.

Ouch. Raine pressed her lips together. Heat pooled in her cheeks.

Forget brainy professor.

He sounded like an intellectual snob.

She stared down her nose at him. "Being a barista is an honorable job."

"Very. I couldn't survive without them. But the position would look odd on my CV."

Tension—thick and heavy—grew between them. CV stood for something in Latin, but she didn't know what. Didn't need to know. She'd worked full-time at coffee shops and barely finished getting her associate's degree.

"You mean, résumé? That's the word this community college graduate uses, Professor." The words spewed like a gallon of French roast had when a spigot on a coffeepot broke. Raine was tired of men who thought they were better than her.

An odd expression formed on his face. "Résumé works."

What else would he say? Raine should stop now. Except, she didn't want to. "I suppose there also might not be room for it with all those fancy degrees and initials after your name. Though master barista is a thing if you change your mind…"

He stared at her as if she'd grown horns.

Maybe she had.

Raine had only been half joking about hiring him. Not that she wouldn't follow through if he'd said yes. His attitude about what she did for a living, however, bugged her. A lot. "But you'd have to pass the food handler's test to get a card. That's required to work here."

He raised his chin. A vein pulsed at his jaw. "How hard

could the test be?"

Not hard at all, but Raine would keep that to herself. She shouldn't try to annoy him. He'd helped her out. She owed him. But what was it with people who thought they were better than everyone else?

Well, her.

She made a smiley face on the foam and handed the drink to him. "This is a pumpkin spice latte. Enjoy."

He stared at the drink. "Never tried one of these."

Keaton didn't sound unsure, more...wary.

"You always order Americanos when I take your order. What made you change your mind?"

"What I've been doing hasn't been working so well. I decided I shouldn't keep doing the same things and should try new things instead."

"Many people need to do that." Herself, included. Maybe she wasn't too old to learn something from an actual professor. "So, how's it going?"

He took a sip. Grinned. "This is delicious, so I'd say it's going well."

Raine stood taller. "You paid for this drink, so your next one is on me. I appreciate you refilling the coffee cup for that customer."

"Not necessary, but thanks." He motioned to an empty table in the corner. "I'll be working over there if you need someone to refill cups. As you've seen, I've got mad pouring skills."

And a massive ego.

Having three older brothers who were a professor, lawyer, and surgeon must have driven Callie crazy. Raine had new respect for her friend, though her siblings might be why the doggy daycare owner preferred dogs to most people.

Raine laughed. "You do."

She wouldn't ask to use those skills of his again. Someone like Keaton Andrews would never lower himself to work in a coffee shop.

For the best.

She was finished with people who thought they were better than others or wanted more than what she loved.

For Emmett, it had been this town until he'd decided she no longer fit into his future. For Keaton, it was her profession.

Why couldn't people see the value in what others appreciated? Why did it have to be their priorities to the exclusion of everyone else's?

She didn't get it.

Chapter Four

A T THE COFFEE shop, Keaton rubbed his eyes. He'd been staring at his computer screen for thirty minutes. His job search showed nothing new while he'd been offline driving to Silver Falls.

I should be teaching my course right now.

It was true, but someone else was doing that.

Which meant his focus was on the job search and his manuscript.

As the first week turned into a second, he'd gotten less picky over the jobs he would apply for. But his holy grail would be a visiting instructor position. That would see him through the school year. A temporary job would give him additional time to look for a permanent spot at a tier-one university. Though after talking to friends at other schools, finding a tenure-track position might be a long shot.

No reason to get discouraged.

Keaton closed his laptop. Today was his first full day in Silver Falls. He couldn't expect a change in location to bring a miracle. Even if deep inside, he wanted that to happen.

Overall, his Monday was going well. He'd stopped off at Taryn's bakery for a cookie and said hello to her staff. Even though Jayden had offered a coffee, Keaton said no. Lawson's couldn't compete with Raine's coffee.

He sipped his drink. Lukewarm but delicious. The pumpkin spice flavoring was growing on him. The smiley face in the milk brought a grin to his face.

Keaton glanced at the counter, but a customer blocked his view of Raine. He'd see her plenty given Tea Leaves and Coffee Beans was where he planned to work on his book. The coffee and the Wi-Fi were as strong as he remembered. And the price was cheaper than in L.A. Good given his current budget.

He downed what remained in his cup.

Might need to order another.

Margot worked at the quilt shop until five. Her dogs—Angus and Sadie—were at Callie's doggy daycare and wouldn't be home until Margot picked them up. That left an empty house for Keaton.

He'd enjoyed the quiet, but after two hours the silence had gotten to him, reminding him of his last day at the university and that he wasn't there for the start of fall quarter. No need to return to the empty house. He might as well work on his book.

Keaton opened his laptop and opened the file.

Mom's suggestion to work on the manuscript had been a good one. The prose was in better shape than he recalled. Most of all, he was proud of what he'd created. He'd started it after that fateful class freshman year changed his major and his life.

The story, a love letter to Norwegian folklore, featured

trolls from *Trold-Tindterne* and the *álfar*. The elves were crucial to the story.

He'd queried an agent to seek representation. Worse come to worse, he could investigate publishing the book himself. After his quest for tenure died a premature death and he'd lost his job, he'd been nothing more than a passenger adrift in the Stadhavet Sea on a boat with no rudder or compass.

He touched his laptop.

But the manuscript had become a lifeline to him, providing direction and giving him another goal to pursue than a new job.

Face it. Writing was better than taking a random job he was overqualified for.

You're so good at this I'm tempted to hand you an apron, and put you to work.

He cringed.

Raine had shocked him by suggesting he'd be a good employee.

Keaton Andrews BA, MA, PhD working as a barista?

Laughable.

Yes, but his reaction had been rude.

He should have said thank you and appreciated her for seeing him as employable. Something his university hadn't done. He'd discovered not all non-tenured faculty in the Scandinavian Studies department had been let go. A couple had been absorbed elsewhere.

But everyone had abandoned him. Ghosted would be the more popular term. His texts and emails got no replies. He'd even tried calling but only got voicemails and no one called him back. Only Lilia stopped by his office to wish him good luck. A scribbled note taped to his former office's door had been his goodbye to the colleagues he'd worked with for six years.

He didn't get it.

No farewell gathering or happy hour to bid him *adieu*.

No card signed by everyone in the department.

No offers to introduce him to others in the field.

He'd become persona non grata. As if by associating with someone let go, they would become tainted.

The only thing Lilia said was that a few people considered him stuffy and egotistical. But that had never been mentioned in his course surveys from students or in his reviews. Yes, he'd been acting the part of a professor, but he'd made sure students found him approachable.

No dwelling on the past.

Keaton had his family in L.A. and in Silver Falls, including Brandt, his aunt Margot, and Taryn.

Another cup with another smiley face appeared in front of him.

He glanced up. "Are you a mind reader?"

The dark circles under Raine's eyes had nothing to do with the mascara and eyeliner she wore. "I read the tea leaves in the last cup I steeped. They said you needed a refill."

He laughed. "I did. Thanks."

She glanced at the counter. No customers were there if that was what she wanted to check.

"I was about to work on something else," he added. "A

book. A fun project not an academic one."

"What does a fun book mean to someone like you?"

His brows creased. "You mean someone who teaches at a college?"

"If the tweed fits…"

He grinned. "Fair enough. I wrote a fantasy novel years ago. I haven't had time to work on it until now."

Her eyes widened. "That's cool. Lots of people say they want to write a book, but you're doing it."

Raine's excitement brought a rush of his own. "I am. I love how the story keeps improving."

"Good luck with it. I hope the drink inspires you to the top of the NYT bestseller list."

He'd love to hit a list someday. He raised his cup in a toast to her.

"Thanks." Keaton took a sip. Another latte. "Very inspiring. I'm enjoying these."

Her smile relaxed, bringing a brightness to her tired eyes and face. Despite her tiredness, Raine was attractive with expressive eyes. Her facial structure would be the envy of social media influencers. But—and it was a big but—her multiple ear piercings and her asymmetrically cut platinum-blond-streaked brunette hair made her one hundred and eighty degrees different from his ideal woman.

He dated girl-next-door or academic types, women who would fit in at university gatherings. Callie claimed he was a snob, only dating women who still wore pearls and sweater sets who would meet a dean's approval. She might be right. Not that dating that type had helped him keep his job.

"I'd better get back to the counter. Wave if you need another," she said. "I'll bring it over if there's no one at the counter."

This was his chance. He set the drink on the table. "I'm sorry for being so rude when you mentioned hiring me."

"Don't worry about it." The way her words shot out belied her casual tone.

No matter what she said, it had mattered to her. He'd hurt her with his careless words.

"I was half joking," she added. "Just getting a little desperate trying to find more help."

He was fighting a bit of desperation himself. His frustration over losing his job had gotten the best of him. Flynn and their parents must be relieved Keaton had left Southern California. "I hope you find someone soon."

"Me, too."

The bell on the door jingled. Brecken, who worked for Taryn, and the barista Keaton remembered serving him this summer walked in.

The only difference from a month ago?

The barista's hair was green instead of purple.

"Hey, Boss," Timmy called out.

A genuine grin crossed Raine's face.

Keaton did a double take. She hadn't smiled at him or other customers like that.

She hugged Timmy. "How did classes go today?"

"Good." Timmy glanced at the counter. "Here alone?"

Raine's nod was imperceptible. Keaton would have missed it if he hadn't been staring at her.

"You're exhausted." Timmy's gaze narrowed. "When was the last time you ate?"

She rubbed her neck. "Um, yesterday. Lunch, I think."

Keaton's mouth dropped open. She thought?

Not good. He felt like an even bigger jerk. She hadn't been kidding about being desperate.

Brecken bit his lip.

Timmy was the only one who didn't appear surprised. "That's what I thought."

"I'm fine." Raine's words sounded practiced, too smooth.

"And I'm the newest member of MENSA." Timmy handed his backpack to Brecken. "I'm taking over the counter for a few minutes, so Raine can take a break."

Brecken nodded.

Funny, but Keaton found himself nodding too.

She shook her head. "That's not necessary."

Timmy put his arm around her shoulder. "Go into the office and close the door. Eat. Take a catnap. Just relax, okay?"

Relief transformed Raine's face yet again, more like the barista Keaton remembered from visits this summer and in December.

Callie spoke highly of Raine, as a friend and a business owner. His sister called Raine strong—a fighter. He expected her to tell Timmy no. Instead, she walked toward the counter with him.

Brecken came closer to Keaton. "Mind if we sit with you? Well, me. Timmy will be here soon enough."

"Go ahead."

He placed the backpacks on the floor and sat in an empty chair at the table. "Taryn said you were back in town."

"I'm staying at Margot's again."

"Yeah, Taryn and Garrett are too into each other. Callie and Brandt too." Brecken's expression was more tween than teen. "Taryn said Raine was working too much, but it's worse than I thought."

"She mentioned trying to hire a barista."

"She needs like three of them. Timmy's working weekends and a couple of nights, but he worked full-time before classes started last month."

"You started college too. How's it going?"

Brecken hung his head as if the weight of the world rested on his eighteen-year-old shoulders. "Community college is so much harder than high school."

"What's difficult about it?"

Brecken wouldn't meet Keaton's eyes. "I got an F on my first paper."

The dejection in the kid's voice reminded Keaton of when he and Flynn had found Brecken after he'd run away. "Did you turn the paper in?"

"Yeah, but I may have watched the movie instead of reading the book."

"May have?"

"Okay, I did." Brecken rubbed his hands over his face. "I was babysitting my brothers and sisters, and time got away from me. I couldn't read the book in one day *and* write a paper."

"What book?"

"*The Scarlet Letter.*"

Keaton winced. The instructor would have known right away.

Brecken leaned forward. "You've read the book and seen the movie?"

"Yes. You can't take shortcuts like that. Not at college."

"It's community college."

"Doesn't matter. A high school English teacher would have caught that." Keaton remembered a meme. It might help Brecken understand. "Picture an iceberg. The part above the water is the movie. The larger portion below the water is the book."

"The book sank the *Titanic.*"

"I suppose you could say that, but with movie adaptions, sometimes the film and the book aren't the same iceberg. They're separated by miles. Sometimes in different oceans."

"Yeah, I guess the ending is different from what I watched." Brecken blew out a breath. "I won't do that again."

Timmy placed an iced coffee with a straw in front of Brecken. "We can study as soon as Raine's back."

"Take your time. I'm catching up with Keaton." Brecken sipped his drink. "So good, thanks."

"If you guys need help with your classes, and it's not a STEM subject, I'm happy to help." Keaton would miss holding office hours.

"Cool." Brecken glanced at Timmy. "Keaton's a professor at a university the smart kids with high test scores go to."

Timmy nodded. "I remember you working on a syllabus

this summer."

Keaton's chest tightened. It took every ounce of strength to keep a smile on his face. "I did."

The word came out stiffer than he'd wanted, but the two young men didn't seem to notice.

The bell on the front door jingled.

"Need to take care of the customer." Timmy raced toward the counter.

"Timmy's a junior at Summit Ridge University." Brecken took another sip. "He's taken a couple of the courses I'm in, so he offered to help me. I'm not much use to him, but you would be."

"Don't say that about yourself. You can be helpful, too. A different perspective can be all that's necessary to learn something new."

"Even if I'm not in his classes?"

At the counter, Raine came out from the back and shooed Timmy away, even though the young man fought her.

That wasn't much of a break. She still appeared tired, but her smile came easier. "Even then."

Chapter Five

KEATON LISTENED TO Brecken and Timmy explain their homework. Timmy had a better grasp of his assignment. Brecken needed better study habits. The start of school was a challenging time for freshmen under the best of circumstances.

"You keep looking at the counter." Timmy closed his textbook. "If you want another latte, I'll get it for you."

"I don't, thanks." Keaton had wanted to see if the line had died down so he could talk to Raine. It hadn't. Not that he knew what he wanted to say.

Keaton had apologized.

Just words.

That was the problem.

How could Keaton show her that he was sorry for acting like a snobby jerk?

The question remained on his mind as he sat at Margot's dining room table. If he'd come across as unapproachable with colleagues, it had been unintentional. He didn't want to leave that impression in Silver Falls, especially not with Raine. He also couldn't erase her look of relief when Timmy offered to help.

"Keaton."

He jolted. "What?"

The five others at the table stared at him. Even Angus and Sadie, who sat close by, waiting to devour anything that dropped to the floor, had their eyes on Keaton.

He took a sip of wine to gather himself.

So what if he was daydreaming?

His family thought he lived too much in his head. Something he'd never denied. Margot, Brandt, and Taryn would figure that out soon enough if they hadn't already.

Callie's gaze narrowed. "You're distracted tonight."

He placed his glass on the table. "Something happened when I was working on my book at the coffee shop. It's been on my mind."

Brandt snickered. "If that's the first place you went in town, you must have missed Raine's Americanos?"

"It was the second place. I got a cookie from the bakery first." Keaton's words had Taryn shimmying her shoulders. "And I drank two pumpkin spice lattes, not an Americano."

His siblings gasped.

"What?" he asked.

Garrett's gaze narrowed. "You always get the same thing."

"Always," Callie echoed. "You're like the sun rising in consistency."

Keaton had been, but... "Not today."

Margot stared over her wineglass at him. Her blue eyes twinkling brighter than ever. "Change is good for the soul."

"Brecken showed up. Timmy too." Keaton didn't want

Callie or Garrett to harp on the change in coffee drinks. "I helped them with homework."

Garrett laughed. "Always the professor."

"It's great to have one in the family. Thank you for helping, Keaton. Brecken's trying so hard, but having dyslexia makes studying difficult for him. He's getting assistance from the school, but I don't know if it's enough." Taryn smiled at him. "Up for more tutoring while you're here?"

Keaton had enjoyed helping the two young men today. "Sure. Especially if that means unlimited baked goods."

Taryn's face brightened. "Happy to work something out with you. And please let me know if Brecken should cut back his work schedule. I want him to succeed."

"Brecken will, sweetheart." Garrett kissed Taryn's cheek. "Because he has you, his family, and all of us on his side."

Margot nearly sighed. Keaton had to admit they were sweet together. He never thought Garrett would ever be so relaxed and not focused on a case 24/7. Taryn brought out the best in him. And who wouldn't want an amazing pastry chef in the family?

"You're right." Taryn scooted closer to Garrett. "Brecken told me Flynn paid for his books."

Callie raised her glass as if making a toast. "That's our big brother. The arrogant surgeon is as generous as he is grumpy."

Keaton and Garrett both laughed. It was true.

"Sam's attending Summit Ridge full-time this semester, but he hasn't cut back his hours yet." Callie lowered her glass and reached for another slice of bread Taryn had brought.

"He seems to be handling it well. I'm sure Brecken will figure out college."

"He will. But Taryn, suggest he talk to Sam. Timmy, too, Raine." Brandt passed the butter to Callie without her asking, and she rewarded him with a huge grin. "Sam's smart and has excellent time-management skills. He might be able to help them navigate being full-time students better."

The warmth flowing through Keaton's veins had nothing to do with the delicious roast beef dinner or red wine. Brandt and Taryn fit perfectly into their family. They wanted to help, aka stick their noses in everyone's business, as much as Keaton's parents and siblings. Keaton took another sip of wine.

"I'm thrilled Timmy finally finished his AA degree. He's talked about transferring to the university for years. I only wish Raine had more help." Margot tossed pieces of roast beef to each of her dogs, who gobbled down the meat. "I'm worried about her."

At least Keaton wasn't the only one concerned about Raine. "She's rundown."

"Exhausted." Taryn's smile disappeared. She stared at her plate. "I feel awful I didn't remember she organized the Valentine dance. It seems like so long ago."

"It was right after Emmett left town," Margot said.

Taryn nodded. "Raine didn't want to celebrate the holiday, but that didn't stop her from throwing herself into the event."

Callie sighed. "I should have remembered, too. Raine wasn't in the mood for hearts and love, but the Valentine's dance was so lovely and romantic."

Garrett kissed the top of Taryn's hand. "Sorry I wasn't here for it."

"Next year." Margot's eyes darkened. "All of us should have remembered, but no one wanted to be in charge of the Boo Bash, and she wasn't at the meeting."

"Doesn't make it right." Taryn's tone was harsher than Keaton had ever heard it.

Garrett shot a surprised glance at his wife.

Margot sighed. "You know the rules."

"No backing out." The other two women said at the same time, sounding unhappy.

"That's a stupid rule." Garrett refilled his water glass from the pitcher. "If Raine ends up in the hospital from exhaustion, you won't have a Boo Bash."

Lines creased Margot's forehead. "No one has ended up in the hospital from running an event."

"Have you seen Raine?" Keaton didn't want to be rude to Margot, but he understood why Taryn was upset. "Timmy told me he's worried Raine will collapse completely. She hadn't eaten since lunch yesterday. He took over the counter long enough for Raine to take a break and eat."

Callie shook her head. "She can't keep up that pace."

"Nope, and I told her that." Taryn ran her fingertips along the stem of her wineglass. "Raine ending up in the hospital might be the only thing to make the association change their rule."

Margot's chin jutted forward. Her eyes darkened to a steely blue. "The rule's in place for a reason. We can't have people walk away from their responsibilities. Trust me, they will. It happened in the past. Then there's a last-minute scramble to put on the event."

Callie stared at Margot. "Do you really think Raine can organize a decent event while working twelve-plus-hour days, seven days a week?"

Margot flinched. "Raine mentioned being short-staffed…"

"It's not just that," Taryn explained. "Even if she hires people, they need to be trained and supervised. She can leave Timmy alone, but not Heather. The woman's too unreliable. So even if Heather shows up, Raine needs to be there."

Callie wiped her mouth with a napkin. "I wasn't a huge fan of Emmett, but at least the guy worked hard and helped out."

"Speaking of Emmett. He texted me this morning to find out if Raine was dating anyone," Brandt said.

Callie's lips parted. "Why didn't you tell me?"

"Sorry. I got busy working on an app and forgot," Brandt admitted. "But I'm telling you now."

She nodded. "Next time text me right away."

"I will." Brandt kissed her forehead. "Promise."

Keaton hadn't gotten to know Brandt all that well, but Rex loved the guy, as did Angus and Sadie, so the dogs' approval was a good sign.

"I don't understand. Emmett is dating a woman in Seattle." Margot scratched her chin. "Why would he ask about Raine?"

"New doesn't always mean better." As Garrett looked at

Taryn his expression softened. "Maybe Emmett realizes what he lost and wants to get back together with Raine."

"They tried dating long distance. Twice." Taryn swirled her glass of wine. "It didn't work. Raine said she wouldn't do that again."

"Long distance isn't the only option," Garrett said. "I ended up here."

Brandt nodded. "And I moved back."

"Emmett told his mother he'll never return to Silver Falls. And we all know Raine would never sell." Margot spoke with authority. "She's built her coffee shop from the ground up."

"A month ago, I would have agreed with you." Callie bit her lip. "But being understaffed and now having to plan the Boo Bash might push her over the edge, so she wants out."

Garrett nodded. "No one would blame her."

Margot's expression scrunched as if she'd drunk a shot of vinegar. "You make it sound like the Boo Bash is the problem. Callie, you've only lived in Silver Falls for three and a half years, but Taryn's been here her entire life. The First Avenue Business Association has rules for a reason."

"This one is unreasonable. Always has been," Taryn countered, not backing down. "There's no reason it can't be changed. Especially when Raine should never have been put up for a vote in the first place. If this keeps up, businesses will choose not to join the association."

Keaton hadn't known his sister-in-law for long, but his respect for Taryn grew. She must keep Garrett on his toes, which was exactly what the former workaholic needed.

Margot harrumphed. "Businesses ask to join the association."

Callie glanced at Brandt. Keaton could see his sister was holding back from the way she bit her lip.

The reason?

Margot was Brandt's aunt.

"Well, this isn't what you want to hear, Margot, but what's happened to Raine is enough to make me reconsider being a member," Callie admitted. "I've been discussing it with Anna, Sam, and Mary Jo."

Margot gasped. "You can't be serious."

"I don't know if the bakery will renew next year. I love the events, especially the Christmas window decorating contest, but many of the rules and fines are unreasonable. Especially now that I have a life outside the bakery." Taryn smiled complete with heart-eyes at Garrett. "We don't have kids yet, but if we do…"

Callie nodded. "I'm sorry, Margot. We're not the only ones thinking that way. Pippa's ready to pull out too. I know the association counts on the flower baskets she makes come springtime."

"That's…" Margot struggled for what to say next. "When I was your age, I ran the quilt shop on my own. I didn't have a manager and only a part-time employee. Even after the association began, the rules were never a burden."

"You founded the association, Aunt Margot. There used to be only a couple events centered around Christmas. Now, the association puts on something every couple of months." Brandt's affection for his aunt was evident in his kind tone.

"That's a lot to ask of business owners. You have a full staff now. Callie and Taryn too. But if it's a burden on them, what do you think it's like for Pippa, who only has one assistant at her flower shop, and Raine with only two part-time employees?"

Keaton didn't know much about the First Avenue Business Association, but the gap between the younger generation of business owners and the founders appeared to be widening.

Garrett stared over his water glass. "Does the association have a backup plan if the committee head can't continue?"

"No one has quit since we implemented the rule." Margot's tone was firm, but she fiddled with her napkin.

Keaton must be missing something. "People must take rules seriously in Silver Falls."

"There's also a fine if you quit," Callie clarified. "A significant one."

A monetary penalty. No wonder why Raine felt forced. No one should be put in that position.

"Everyone's overlooking something more important than the Boo Bash or any of the other annual events the association puts on." Taryn's voice sharpened. "If Raine burns out and sells Tea Leaves and Coffee Beans, it'll be a huge loss to Silver Falls. I sell coffee, but it's nothing like hers. That means hoping someone else takes over or coffee lovers will have to drive to Summit Ridge."

"A loss to the town, yes. But Raine's a master barista," Callie said, which surprised Keaton. "She can find a job anywhere and not have to deal with staffing issues or the association."

Margot cleared her throat. "We'll bring this up at the October association meeting."

Surprise flashed on Taryn and Callie's faces. Even Brandt's eyes widened.

"In the meantime, Raine needs help," Margot continued.

Taryn nodded. "None of us have time."

"One of us has a little more time." The way Margot's gaze zeroed in on Keaton made him gulp. "Keaton's here for an extended stay. I propose he helps Raine with the Boo Bash."

All eyes at the table shot to him.

The reasons he should say no—looking for a job, working on his book—ran through his head, crashing into one another until his thoughts were a jumbled mess. *No* sat on the tip of his tongue ready to launch into the world.

Keaton glanced at Callie.

Big mistake.

The hope in his baby sis's gaze nearly knocked him out of his chair. She wanted him to help her friend. He'd never been good at saying no to Callie. Not when they'd been kids and not now as adults.

That meant one thing.

He swallowed. "So…what exactly is the Boo Bash?"

Chapter Six

TUESDAY MORNING, RAINE walked along First Avenue with a spring in her step. Not all the tension had seeped away, but enough so her muscles felt looser and more relaxed than they'd been in weeks. Not waking up before the sun helped. She'd had no idea how much she needed a break—if only a few hours off—until now.

Raine couldn't explain the difference, but her senses felt sharper. Heightened. Creativity, something she'd struggled with lately, had woken up. Ideas popped in her head. She wanted to experiment with tea blends and find new ways to use pumpkin spice in coffee drinks.

Even the sun appeared brighter and the sky bluer. Dread no longer gnawed at her gut. Having the feeling disappear gave her hope she would survive until the Boo Bash.

Four weeks to the day.

That wasn't too much to ask.

She had one person to thank for giving her the time to regroup.

Her lazy morning, what she called not having to wake up until seven, was courtesy of Timmy, who deserved another raise for offering to open the shop in case Heather called out.

His class didn't start until nine, an hour from now.

Raine inhaled, filling her lungs with the crisp September air. She couldn't wait for the temperatures to cool so she could bring out her comfy, big sweaters and knit caps. She wanted to thrive and enjoy autumn.

Given she hadn't enjoyed winter, spring, or summer, it was time.

"Good morning, Raine," Mr. Jones called from the sidewalk outside his hardware store. He held on to a broom. "It's a beautiful day."

"Yes, it is." A decent night's sleep and a full breakfast with protein—in her case eggs—changed her entire outlook. "Have a good one."

"You, too." He rested against the broom handle. "Hope the Boo Bash planning is coming along."

Reality crashed down on her, like a pallet full of candy dropped onto her head. She nearly stumbled, falling face first on the cement, until she stuck her arms out to catch her balance.

Her pulse sprinted as if running away from a guy in a hockey mask carrying a bloodstained machete.

She took a breath and another.

Her breathing evened out. So did her heart rate.

Raine didn't answer Mr. Jones. She continued to her coffee shop. But now, her shoulders hunched, and her head wanted to hide like a turtle in its shell. Her steps plodded. She opened the door and nearly bumped into Robin Baxter, standing in line.

Seeing so many people waiting at this hour surprised her.

Yes, eight o'clock was the height of rush hour, but the line reminded her of the crowds during the summer fair, when people wanted to escape the July heat with cool air and a cold drink in the coffee shop.

Timmy prepared drinks at a speedy pace, but parts of the process couldn't be rushed.

Raine hurried behind the counter. "Where's…"

He motioned to the back. "I'm moving as fast as I can. They all came at once. Sorry."

"You're doing a great job." One person could only do so much, which was why she preferred having two people there if possible. "I'll drop off my stuff, wash my hands, and be right out."

Plus, she wanted to see why Heather wasn't out front. The woman had better have a good reason for taking a break now.

The door to the office was ajar.

Laughter sounded.

Raine went closer to the door, but she didn't open it.

"No, I don't have to get back to work." Heather laughed again. "What's Raine going to do? Fire me?"

Raine couldn't see Heather's face, but she imagined a cackling, evil clown drawing polka dots on the shop apron with a marker.

"She needs me. That's why I can come and go as I please. Work when I want to and blow off shifts when I choose. I've got this position locked down."

Raine's muscles tensed, tightening into small cannon balls she wanted to fire at Heather.

Strike that, she wanted to fire Heather.

"Nope. Raine can't hire anyone else. Each time she makes an appointment to interview someone, I call them back and say position's been filled." Heather snickered. "Like I said. Locked down. Solid. Indispensable."

Raine's blood pressure spiraled into the red zone. So did her temper. Desperation had put her in this place, but she'd never thought Heather would take advantage of Raine this way.

"Now, I need to figure out how to get a raise."

Raine's hands balled. She considered herself a relatively calm person, more go-with-the-flow than in someone's face. But her blood boiled. She was ready to erupt like Mount Saint Helens.

She pushed open the door. "Hang up the phone. Now."

"Gotta go." Heather's words ran together. She disconnected from the call and smiled. The plastic grin would have looked phony on a doll. "Hey. I didn't think you were going to be in until eight."

"It's after eight."

Heather blushed. Not unexpected given the circumstances, but the woman, who was in her mid-twenties, should have known she would get caught eventually.

"Guess I should get out front." Heather took a step toward the door.

Raine blocked her. "You're fired."

Heather's jaw dropped. "Say what?"

"You're fired." Repeating the words didn't lessen the knots in Raine's shoulders. Breathing, however, came easier.

"Get your things and clock out. You'll get your final check next Friday."

"B-b-but… I had to take that call. It was important."

"I hope so because it's the last you'll ever take here."

Heather scoffed. "You can't fire me. You can't run this place without me."

"I've been running it without you, and now that I know you're the reason no one's showed up for their interviews, I have a feeling I won't be alone much longer."

As if on cue, crocodile tears shot from Heather's eyes. They streamed down her face in black mascara-tinged streaks. "Please don't fire me. I need this job."

No apology. Just how this affected Heather.

Raine's final breakup with Emmett had been that way, as if she weren't a participant in the conversation—or their relationship. His wants and needs had been the only topic.

Raine raised her chin. "You should have thought about that before you chose to play games. Don't use me as a reference unless you want me to tell them the truth."

She wanted to say more, but she held back. Heather hadn't acted like an adult. Raine wouldn't make the same mistake.

"Get your things, clock out, and leave." Raine kept her voice steady and professional. "If you won't, I'll call the sheriff."

Heather sneered, her face squishing up like a cartoon villain. "You wouldn't."

Raine stared down her nose. She didn't blink. "Try me."

Heather stood there as if considering it. Then, she huffed

and went to the employee lockers to remove her jacket and purse.

Raine watched Heather's every move. She'd forgotten something. "Take off your apron."

Heather nearly ripped off the waist ties, pulled the apron's neck strap over her head, wadded the fabric into a ball, and threw it against the floor.

"You can have it." Spit flew out of her mouth. "I wouldn't want the ugly thing anyway."

Heather held on to her things, clocked out, and rushed out of the office.

As Raine put away her purse and tied a clean apron around her waist, she peered out the door.

Heather remained behind the counter. "Raine fired me. Can you believe she fired me?"

"About time." Timmy didn't glance her way. He set a drink on the counter. "Pippa."

The florist, who wore a cheery daisy-print dress, stepped up. "If you'd worked for me, I would have let you go a month ago."

The crowd in line murmured their agreement.

Heather harrumphed on her way out of the shop, nearly ripping the front door off its hinges. As soon as the door closed and the bells stopped ringing, everyone in line applauded.

Raine hadn't been expecting that reaction. She joined Timmy. "Guess I was wrong thinking customer service would suffer without Heather."

"If you weren't here, Heather barely helped." Timmy

made a herringbone design in a latte. "You kept saying you needed her, so I figured you saw something in her that I didn't."

Idiot. Keeping Heather had only made things worse. "I should have trusted my gut."

"Next time. She's gone now." Timmy placed the drink on the counter. "Anna."

Anna, the dog groomer who worked for Callie, stepped up and grabbed her drink. "You got rid of a dead weight. Don't think twice about firing her. She deserved it."

With that, Anna left.

Good advice. Raine glanced at the clock. It was later than she thought. "I'll wash my hands so you can get to class. I don't want you to be late."

"Take your time." Timmy worked on the next drink. "I have a few minutes."

Raine returned two minutes later to find Timmy had gotten through more of the line, but a few customers still needed to order. "Thanks for opening today. Now go."

"See you this afternoon, Boss." Timmy went into the back.

Two minutes later, on his way out the front door with his backpack on, he waved.

As soon as things slowed, Raine would call the applicants who she'd thought ghosted her, explain the situation, and ask if they were interested in interviewing. But that still left her with…

Hope the Boo Bash planning is coming along.

Nope. Not thinking about that today. She hadn't even

had time to open the bin Margot had dropped off and the first of October was only three days away.

Raine finished the caramel macchiato Timmy had been working on. She placed the cup on the counter. "Lyndsey."

She returned to the cash register.

Robin Baxter stepped forward. Her chin quivered. "H-hello."

Raine had to ask. "You okay?"

"Thought about the job." Robin bit her lip—something Raine had never seen the normally flawlessly put-together woman do. "If you're still hiring, I'm...interested in applying. I'm a quick learner and free to work after I drop off the kids at school until they get out. And I can work other shifts depending on when Nick has Savannah and Nicky."

Raine's gut screamed to hire her on the spot. She wouldn't ignore the instinct this time. "You're hired."

Robin flinched. "Just like that?"

Raine nodded. "If you can stick around, I have paperwork for you to fill out. But it'll be a few minutes until I can get it."

Robin laughed. "I'd rather hang out here than go home and try to keep everything spotless in case a real estate agent has a showing."

Raine fixed a quick coffee with cream and sugar. She handed the cup to Robin. "Have a seat. I'll be with you as soon as I can."

One employee fired, one hired. That helped. Now to find at least two more.

She smiled. "Welcome to Tea Leaves and Coffee Beans.

What can I get you?"

Keaton Andrews stood there. His laptop bag hung off his shoulder. "Your smile's a great start."

Her breath caught. She must still be trying to calm down after Heather.

"Hey. I didn't see you come in." Raine had been focused on making sure Heather left. "Sorry for the wait."

"Not a problem. Quite a morning you've had."

"How much did you see?"

"Enough. You okay?" Keaton asked, his tone concerned.

"Yes." But her staffing issues might be behind her. A warm, fuzzy feeling, as if she'd sipped a hot cocoa drizzled with hot fudge sauce and candy cane sprinkles, flowed through her. "An Americano this morning?"

"I want to try another pumpkin spice drink. Something different from the lattes yesterday."

"There's plenty to choose from on the menu."

"Surprise me again."

"Living dangerously?"

"It appears so."

She ran through the pumpkin spice drinks. "I know exactly what you need."

"And so do I." His face reddened. "I mean what you need."

Her heart thudded.

Whoa.

That was a strange reaction. Keaton's words sounded a little flirty. But he wouldn't, would he?

His smile wavered. "I want to offer my services."

The words hung in the air between them.

Raine thought she'd heard him correctly but maybe not. "Your what?"

"My services."

O-kay. Except it wasn't. "You lost me. Not surprising given you're a professor and I'm me, but what services?"

Because after yesterday, she couldn't imagine him working for her as a barista. *Strike that.* She could imagine it. He couldn't. Wouldn't. Of that, she was one hundred percent certain.

"At dinner with my family the Boo Bash came up," he clarified.

"You mean, the thorn in my side."

"How would you like help pulling out that thorn?"

She was missing something. It wouldn't be the first time given how long she'd missed the signs of Emmett's unhappiness in Silver Falls and with her. "Huh?"

"I want to help you organize the Boo Bash."

The words rushed out as if he were nervous, so much that Boo Bash sounded like one word. The result was adorable.

He adjusted his glasses. "That is, if you want help organizing it."

"Are you kidding? They gave me a bin of stuff, and I haven't opened it. The event is four weeks away, but I have no idea where to start. No time…"

It was her turn for the words to gush out one on top of another. She didn't care. An unlikely hero was stepping in, and she couldn't be more grateful.

"I'd love your help. Like love it so much you're my new best friend, and I want to name a tea blend or coffee drink after you."

He laughed. "There's no need for the latter, but a person can never have too many friends."

She nodded, back and forth as if her head had turned into a rocking chair. "Like I said we have some time…"

"I'm the planning type so what if we get started sooner rather than later?"

Raine needed the help. Somehow, she would have to make time to work on the Boo Bash. "Sure, when?"

"Today."

She swallowed.

He laughed. "Don't look so worried. The Boo Bash doesn't have to be built in a day, but it'll be October soon."

"I didn't realize I looked worried."

"When your eyebrows draw together, little lines form above your nose. That suggests worrying. Or at least contemplation. And not in a positive way."

"No one's mentioned that before." She touched the spot to double-check. "I was worrying."

"Stop. You're no longer on your own."

With each of his words, her stress lessened.

"I'm working here this morning," Keaton continued. "When things slow down, we can discuss the first steps. How does that sound?"

Like she wanted to drop to her knee and propose on the spot.

Okay, not really, they were too different, but a part of

her was in shock. The other part would be eternally grateful to him. "Sure. Sounds great. Thanks. Your drinks are on the house."

That was the least she could do.

Reality, however, wouldn't let her enjoy this unexpected windfall.

A little voice inside her kept her suspicions on high alert.

What does a professor know about Halloween? Why would he offer to do that after dissing baristas yesterday?

Unfortunately, another voice answered back.

Margot.

Raine didn't like that.

Not at all.

Chapter Seven

THE NUMBER OF customers didn't slow. If anything, more arrived. Good for the bottom line, but Raine's stress level inched up with every drink she made. Juggling the orders was easy, but she hated keeping Robin and Keaton waiting.

They didn't seem to mind.

At tables next to each other, the two sat and talked. Keaton's smile after each sip suggested he enjoyed the Pumpkin Spice Caramel Macchiato.

Satisfaction flowed through Raine. She wanted all her customers to enjoy their drinks, but Keaton had stepped outside his wheelhouse these past two days.

Not an Americano in sight.

Trying a different beverage might not sound like a big deal, but for some customers, it was huge. They preferred their favorite and never switched no matter how many free samples she offered. And she'd tried with many.

She placed an apple cider into a drink tray with other coffees for the fire station. "Rachelle."

The beautiful firefighter came to the counter. Her box braids made her look like a model or movie star. Her black skin was radiant, matching her bright smile. Pregnancy agreed with Rachelle. Her baby bump hadn't kept her from being promoted in the fire department.

"Don't tell Jayden I came here." Rachelle glanced around and lowered her voice. "He claims the bakery's coffee is as good as yours, but we both know the truth."

Raine grinned. This wouldn't be the first time a loyal customer asked her to not mention being in the coffee shop. "Your secret is safe with me."

Rachelle picked up the drink tray and headed out.

As soon as the bell stopped jingling, Raine dashed into the office, grabbed the new hire folder, and set it on top of the orange and black bin. She carried everything to the sitting area and placed the bin on the empty chair at Keaton's table. "Sorry it took me so long."

"No need to apologize." Keaton placed his cup on the table. "I've been enjoying my drink while Robin told me about the Boo Bash."

"It's my kids' favorite event of the year." Robin was smiling now. "I thought the Easter egg hunt would be their number one, but they can't stop talking about the Boo Bash."

"Everyone loves candy." Keaton laughed. "My oldest brother is a surgeon. He always has a bag of peanut M&Ms with him. The only place it doesn't go is into the operating room."

Robin grinned. "That's sweet."

"Literally," Keaton joked.

Raine had forgotten the oldest brother's name. Finn. No,

Flynn. The doctor was shorter than Keaton and had an intense personality like Garrett. Maybe Keaton did, too. She didn't know him beyond his visits to the coffee shop, a rehearsal dinner, and a wedding.

He didn't seem like the joke-cracking kind, but she might have stereotyped him as a geeky professor after hearing Callie talk about her brainy brother. He'd shown Raine he could also be stuffy and stuck up. She'd accepted his apology. Forgetting would take longer.

His offer to help caught her off guard. She hadn't fully recovered, but she needed to try. "Do you carry candy with you, Professor?"

"No, candy, but I carry this." Keaton reached into his pocket and pulled out keys. He held up a keychain—a rounded metal piece that was crossed. "This is made from iron and called a *trollkor* or troll cross. It wards off trolls and other evil creatures."

Raine raised a brow. "Come across those often?"

"No. Must work," he teased.

Robin laughed. So did Raine.

"A student gave me this as a thank you. A *trollkor* is usually placed above a door or window. Mine was above my bedroom window." He placed his keys next to his drink. "Before I left for Silver Falls, I added it to my keychain."

Raine couldn't resist. "Got to keep the trolls away."

"Evil little creatures. Though size doesn't matter. There are other mischievous ones out." Amusement filled his voice. "Big and small."

The troll comments were funny, but Raine got the feeling sentimentality was the real reason he carried the *trollkor*. Callie was like that. But hearing Keaton mention trolls gave Raine hope. Maybe working on the Boo Bash wasn't that big of a leap for him.

"Learn something new every day," she quipped.

Keaton's smile slid into a smirk. "I know what you're thinking."

It was her turn to grin. "Does the *trollkor* give you telepathic abilities?"

"No, your face does."

She touched between her eyebrows but felt no lines. "What do you see this time?"

Robin's gaze bounced between Keaton and Raine. She sipped her coffee.

Keaton's glasses only magnified his clear and warm green eyes. Not that she was paying close attention to his eyes. Or to him. Not that close anyway.

"Curiosity," he said finally.

Okay, Raine was curious. "You're good at this."

"Fifty-five percent of communication is nonverbal." His professor tone annoyed her less today. "Understanding my students' body language and deciphering their tones helps me to teach better."

She lifted her chin. "What did my body language tell you?"

He rubbed his chin. "You want to know how I'll help with a Halloween community event?"

Her mouth dropped open. "I do."

His gaze pierced through her as if her secrets were on full

display to him. She shifted her weight between her feet, wishing she hadn't set down the bin.

He kept staring at her. Her temperature shot up twenty degrees. She wanted to fan herself.

"It's a valid question," he admitted. "Do you know the answer?"

Robin's arm shot into the air as if she were a student. "I know the answer."

"Go ahead." Raine wanted to take back some control.

"Keaton teaches folklore, legends, and mythology," Robin said.

He gave a thumbs-up to Robin who beamed. "That makes me a font of holiday trivia and knowledge."

Holidays encompassed a lot. Raine had to ask. "Including Halloween?"

He bowed. "But of course."

"Halloween comes from a mix of traditions and tales. Kids love that stuff. At least mine do," Robin said. "This parent would appreciate the Boo Bash being less about trick-or-treating at First Avenue Businesses and more about the holiday itself. They get enough candy when they go door-to-door in the neighborhood on the thirty-first."

Splat.

That was the sound of Raine's hopes and dreams for an easy event hitting the cement floor beneath her feet.

"Don't worry. Raine and I will come up with something unique and...fun." The way Keaton said the last word sounded almost foreign to him.

Uh-oh. Was having a worthless helper better than no

help at all? If he turned into another Heather...

Not wanting to think about a worst-case scenario, Raine grabbed the file off the top of the bin and patted the plastic lid with her free hand.

"This is what the First Avenue Business Association gave me. Everything I...we...need to plan the Boo Bash is inside."

"I'll check it out."

That would be his first test. Raine hoped he passed it. "If trolls are inside, I'm sure your keychain will make them spontaneously combust."

Laughter lit his eyes. "Let's hope they don't make a mess."

Her heart bumped.

Huh? That reaction made no sense.

She handed paperwork to Robin. "If you want to start training tomorrow after you drop off the kids, bring all the paperwork back filled out and your social security card with you. If you can't tomorrow, let me know what day works for you. This week would be best, but I know this is sudden."

"Thank you." Robin crinkled one of the edges. She smoothed it out. "Thank you so much. I'm so happy to have a job. I'll be here tomorrow."

"Don't you want to know the hourly wage or what you'll be doing?" Raine asked.

"I saw your ad. It had both those things listed. Both are great." Robin gathered her purse and empty cup. "Oh, I forgot one thing. Casual dress?"

"Yes, you'll wear an apron over your clothes, but spills

happen. Jeans, a T-shirt, and closed-toe shoes are standard around here."

Robin stood. "See you in the morning."

She took her cup with her.

Keaton watched Robin leave. "It's hard to believe a narcissist like Nick Baxter has such a sweet wife."

"Soon-to-be ex-wife. Now where were we?"

"Opening this bad boy." Keaton hadn't reached for the bin's lid. "I wonder if this sense of anticipation is what the archeologist in Trondheim felt when they discovered a skeleton at the bottom of an old castle well."

Professors had an odd sense of humor. Unless that was purely Keaton. "A troll skeleton?"

"Human." His grin took ten years off his face, and her pulse kicked up. "In addition to holidays, I'm a font of useless facts about my favorite culture. Norway, in case you didn't guess."

"I hadn't. Do you have family ties to the country?"

"Nope. Even did one of the DNA tests. I fell in love with the country my freshman year of college in a course on Old Norse folklore. Until then I'd been a philosophy major and pre-law."

"One class changed everything?"

"It did."

"You were lucky to find your passion early."

"When did you discover coffee?"

"I used to fix it for my dad. I got my first job as a barista when I was in high school."

"You were younger than me."

Raine nodded, trying to find a way to ask the question on her mind. She rubbed the back of her neck.

"What else do you want to know?"

He was too good at this body language stuff. "There is one thing I'm curious about."

That brow of his shot up. "Only one?"

She didn't want to be amused by him, but she was. "Did Margot pressure you to volunteer for the Boo Bash?"

"She mentioned you needed help, which is why I offered. I'm in town through October at least. I don't have a business to run. And you need help with the Boo Bash. Now, you have it. What's your other question?"

Raine's body language must have given her away again. "Do you have event planning experience?"

"In my department, the newest faculty members help with events. Not large-scale ones, but I have a surprising amount of 'event'..." he made air quotes "...experience. Outside of work, I planned Garrett's bachelor party. Not a family-friendly event though."

"Wait. How did you have a bachelor party when he and Taryn surprised everyone and eloped?"

"It was a post-elopement bachelor..." Keaton rubbed his chin. "Let's call it a groom party since they'd said, 'I do.'"

Why hadn't Raine thought of doing something like that? Probably because she'd been overwhelmed then too. "We should have thrown Taryn a wife shower."

"It's not too late."

"True. Though ordering dessert would have to be done sneakily. Maybe once I hire more people and get past the

Boo Bash."

"Remember, no more thorn in your side. Unless you think I'll be one."

"I'll have to let you know." Raine was cautiously hopeful, but Keaton could turn out to be an even bigger thorn.

He reached for the lid. "Ready to see what's inside?"

SO MUCH FOR opening the bin.

The bell on the door didn't stop jingling. Keaton sat at the table, waiting for Raine to finish with the rush of customers that appeared. He was here to help so he didn't mind waiting.

Keaton could open the bin himself, but where was the fun in that? He pulled out his laptop to work on his manuscript. His gaze, however, kept straying to Raine. He hated the change in her.

As more people stood in line, weariness creeped back into her face, and her smiled turned forced.

All he wanted to do was grab an apron and help her out.

What was wrong with him?

He couldn't do that after what he'd said yesterday. She'd laugh in his face and rightly so. Still, he snuck another peek in her direction.

The tip of her tongue stuck out between her teeth. Whatever she did behind the counter—he couldn't see her hands—she was focused on the task.

Hard at work as usual.

Raine was different from the women he knew. She kept

glancing his way. Not an is-he-a-serial-killer look either. Her gaze lingered longer than it should, and he enjoyed that, more than he should. If she didn't appear so wary, he might think they were in one of those rom-com movies Callie enjoyed watching.

Uh-oh. If he weren't careful, Margot would think her matchmaking scheme was working. Still, his volunteering to help with the Boo Bash had been a good idea.

Raine hurried over. She placed a plate with a cookie on it and another coffee on the table. "This is for you. Sorry to make you wait again."

"Not a problem. I've been working."

"On your book?"

He nodded.

She eyed the lid on the bin. "You didn't open the bin?"

"It's taking all my patience not to open this bad boy. I was the one who found all the Christmas presents my parents hid, but they blamed Callie." Keaton patted the lid. "But I was good. I didn't peek. I wanted to wait for you."

"That's..." She wiped her hands on her apron. "Thank you."

"I have nowhere to be today." Or any day. Which was odd and disconcerting and a million other things Keaton wanted to forget. "But we should open this before someone else needs a coffee."

She remained standing. "Go for it."

He opened the lid. No trolls or remnants of trolls. Only folders, checklists, a clipboard, orange cardstock, and spools of Halloween-themed ribbon. "Is this what you expected?"

She peered over his shoulder. "Honestly, this is more than I thought would be in there. When I got the folder for the Valentine's dance, it didn't have much information. Organizers are so tired and behind they only have time to pass on the basics."

He rifled through the bin. A whole lot of nothing. "That seems to be the case here."

"You sound disappointed. What were you hoping to find?"

"A magical document with a step-by-step of what to do that would make parents, kids, and business owners happy."

"Perfect answer, Professor."

She wasn't making fun of him. Only his family and Margot knew about how he'd lost his job, but hearing Raine call him that burned. His ego had to get used to it.

"Find anything good?" Raine asked.

"A few supplies." Nothing jumped out at him as being particularly helpful. "I'll go through everything, so we know what we have to work with."

How hard could helping Raine be?

Planning a Halloween event for kids was a far cry from translating ancient manuscripts, so fragile they might disintegrate at any moment.

Except the lines on Raine's forehead deepened to Grand Canyon-level depths. His answers to her questions hadn't been enough.

Okay, Keaton got it.

Planning a happy hour, a lunch, or a bachelor party weren't the same as organizing a community event, but what he didn't know, he could learn. She would see. Until then...

He might as well say the words. "I won't be a burden."

Keaton agreed with Robin. The Boo Bash shouldn't be all about the candy. He wouldn't suggest over-the-top, time-intensive ideas, which was likely what Raine expected him to do. "I never called you that."

"No, but the thought crossed your mind?"

Her cheeks reddened.

"No apology necessary," he added quickly. "I don't blame you for thinking that."

Keaton didn't. Robin's comment about not as much candy had dropped the metaphorical guillotine on Raine's neck. Her eyes had gleamed, and her lips trembled slightly. He thought she might cry.

But she hadn't.

When Callie shed tears, Keaton and his brothers did what they could to make the waterworks stop. They hated seeing her hurting, and that had led to more than one trip to various theme parks in the area. Same with Taryn when Brecken had taken off.

Keaton would have done the same with Raine. Not that she would have asked for anything from him. "I just want to help you with the Boo Bash, but you're in charge."

She wet her lips.

He stared at her mouth before glancing at the cookie she'd brought him. "What do you say?"

"Okay. I'm not trying to be a pain. I'm just..."

"Over your head."

The bell on the door jingled.

"Way over." Raine closed her eyes and sighed. "I've—"

"Go."

As she hurried to the counter, he watched her go. The barista didn't fight fires like Jayden's wife, Rachelle, who he'd seen on his way in, but both women were strong. Raine faced a rough time, but she wasn't folding or asking to be rescued. She wanted help, but only the right help.

His type or not, that strength appealed to him at a gut level.

Thirty minutes later, Keaton carried the bin and computer bag to the counter. "I went through everything. I have ideas I'd like to go over with you. Are you free tonight?"

"That soon?"

"The most helpful info in the bin was about purchasing the candy. You can get a discount, but there's a deadline to order."

"The budget isn't big so a discount would help. I can meet later tonight."

She sounded hesitant.

Keaton didn't want to add to her to-do list. "Sure?"

Raine nodded. "Timmy works tonight. I need to be here for some of his shift, but he won't mind closing on his own."

Keaton remembered she hadn't been eating much. "Want me to bring food?"

"I'll grab something for us. You're the volunteer."

Yeah, this wasn't a date. Keaton wouldn't date a woman like Raine, but... "You're a conscripted volunteer."

"More like the fool who keeps renewing her membership in the First Avenue Business Association. This is on me,

Professor. I'll be home around seven. Show up any time after that."

"I need your address." He handed her his phone. "Text it to yourself, so I have your phone number."

She typed on his phone and handed it back. "Pizza, okay?"

"Just no anchovies or pineapple."

"I can live with that."

"I want to go through some of the checklists again." Keaton raised the box. "Mind if I take it with me?"

"It's all yours." Her gaze bounced from the bin to him. "I'm sure this isn't what you thought you'd be doing in Silver Falls…"

"No, but I'm happy to help. Callie and Garrett love Silver Falls. This is for them too."

Raine didn't say anything, but something flashed in her eyes.

Keaton didn't know what. "The town means a lot to you too."

"Yeah." She glanced out the front window. "I searched all over for a place to open my coffee shop. As soon as I visited Silver Falls, I knew this was it."

"It?"

"Home."

Talk about déjà vu. "Callie said something similar after her first visit to Silver Falls."

A wistful expression crossed Raine's face, one so different than any Keaton had seen he wanted to take a picture. He blinked, and it was gone.

She nodded. "Most people who move here feel that way."

"Not sure Garrett did."

Another nod. "But Taryn's here so…"

Brandt had returned to his hometown too. "Love makes people do the unexpected."

He expected her to agree with him not shrug.

She blew out a breath. "Sometimes love isn't enough to make someone stay."

Was she talking about her ex? That Emmett guy? Raine sounded resigned, not hurt.

Still… "Then maybe the love…the person…wasn't the right one."

Gratitude shone in Raine's eyes. "Maybe."

Not that Keaton knew for certain. He wasn't sure if he'd ever been in love or simply infatuated. There seemed to be a fine line. At least for him. But for Raine's sake, he wanted to be correct. And hoped he was.

Chapter Eight

ONCE AGAIN, RAINE owed Timmy. She parked her car in the garage, grabbed the pizza from the passenger seat, and hurried into the house. He was only twenty-two, but he was an old soul. She'd recognized that quality in him when she hired him four years ago and seen it tonight when he'd told her to leave the coffee shop at six thirty because he had everything under control.

Timmy did.

Thank goodness because she needed a shower before Keaton arrived.

Inside, she kicked her shoes off. The clogs went flying and hit the wall.

Oops.

She'd put them in the basket later.

Raine tossed her keys and purse on the kitchen counter. She shoved the pizza box into the oven and set the temperature to warm.

The microwave clock read six fifty.

That gave her ten minutes to shower and change.

If Keaton was punctual. But something—her gut or a hunch—told her he might be early.

That meant a super-short shower.

She ran into her bathroom where she turned on the shower so the water could heat up. All she needed was time to wash off the grime from working all day. She didn't need to put on makeup or do her hair. This was a working dinner, not a date, right?

Right.

As fast as she could, Raine showered, dried off, and dressed. Leggings and a shirt. She wanted to be comfortable after a long day at the shop.

She combed her wet hair.

The doorbell rang.

Not quite seven.

Early as she expected.

A good thing she hadn't planned on makeup because she had no time for that.

Raine walked to the front door and opened it.

Keaton stood there with a pink box from Lawson's bakery on top of the Boo Bash container. Okay, the guy had manners. If he wasn't carrying the orange and black box, this would be a good start to a date. If she wanted a date, which she didn't.

She clutched the doorknob. "You didn't have to bring dessert."

His mouth quirked. "Knew you'd say that."

"But I'm glad you did."

Surprise flashed on his face. "You're welcome."

Catching him off guard felt better than it should. She let go of the door. "I'd be an even bigger fool to say no to something from Lawson's."

"You're not a fool."

She motioned him inside. "Where are my manners? Come in."

He did. "Nice place. I like the wood floors and crown moldings."

"Thanks. I had them redone before I moved in, but I fell in love with all the built-ins and little touches."

"Lots of character." He glanced around. "No dog?"

"Nope." She motioned him inside. "Callie and Anna keep telling me to get a dog or a cat, but I'm not at home enough."

"Surprised they accept that answer given they could look after your dog at Wags and Tails. Callie's been on me about it too."

"Considering it?"

"A Norwegian Elkhound is in my future. I thought perhaps this Christmas, but I need to push out the date."

Raine wanted to know why the timing mattered so much, but it was none of her business. "Norwegian Elkhound? You're really into Norway stuff, huh?"

"Scandinavian studies is my specialty, and those dogs are amazing." Excitement brimmed in his voice. "Perfect disposition for a family."

"I haven't investigated breeds yet, but I can't see adopting a pet, only to put them in doggie daycare seven days a week. Callie's is the only one in the area, and even if I wanted to use them, they aren't open late enough anyway. Or at least they won't be until they start their overnight boarding service."

The way he studied Raine made her want to take cover. "Sounds like you've done some research."

Raine shrugged. That was better than admitting she'd found the perfect dog, but when she asked Emmett to go to the rescue shelter with her, he broke up with her instead. Now she didn't have him, and some other family had provided a forever home for that sweet dog. "A little. Before…"

Uh-oh. She didn't want to talk about that.

Keaton set the dessert on the counter. "Before…"

"Before my ex-boyfriend and I broke up. He lived in an apartment, but I had this house with a fenced yard. He didn't work as much as me, so we'd discussed getting a dog, but then…"

"He decided Silver Falls wasn't the place for him, and he moved to Seattle."

The words seemed to float between them for a long moment. Raine hated every passing second.

Keaton leaned against the counter and crossed one ankle over the other. "So, no dog and no relationship."

It wasn't a question, but Raine felt the need to answer before she changed the subject. "Yep."

That was all Raine would say. Her dating history had nothing to do with planning the Boo Bash. Besides, all he had to do was ask Callie, Taryn, or Margot if he had any questions. Everyone in town knew about the breakup. Margot must know the most, maybe even more than Raine, given the quilt owner's friendship with Mrs. Wilson, Emmett's mom. The fact Raine was never told to call her Teresa probably should have been a warning sign that the relationship would never last. If only hindsight equaled premonition. That would stop a lot of heartache.

Raine opened a drawer, pulled out an oven mitt, and put it on. She pulled the pizza box out of the oven. "I got half a meat lover on one side and pepperoni and olives on the other."

"Excellent choices. I like both."

Keaton's approval made her feel as if she'd earned a gold star. His students must feel the same way when they scored well on a paper or exam. She wondered if some had crushes on the handsome professor. None of her instructors at the community college had caught her eye, but she'd also been working two jobs so didn't have much time for romance.

She placed the box on a trivet. "I just need to get plates."

He came up to her, making the galley kitchen seem even smaller. "Can I help with anything?"

Raine wanted him to move away from her. The woody scent of his soap or aftershave swirled around her head. She liked the smell, something she hadn't noticed at the coffee shop.

"Do you mind getting glasses from the cabinet next to the sink?" She pointed to the one she meant. "There's iced tea in the fridge and ice in the freezer if you want some."

"Do you?"

"No, thanks. It'll be cold enough for me."

For two people who didn't know each other, they worked well in the space they had, staying out of each other's way and setting the table without any issues. The silence wasn't awkward. She appreciated Keaton for not having to fill every second with words like Emmett did.

It was also weird to have a man in her house. The last time had been July when Emmett picked up his boxes. She wasn't an introvert or a recluse, but she'd become that when not working.

How had that happened?

Going out alone isn't much fun.

Come November, Raine needed to do something about that. Not date. The idea of joining a dating app made her nauseous, but maybe she would arrange a girls' night with her friends. They used to have those. Callie and Taryn had their husbands now, but Anna and Pippa were single too.

"I'm ready," he said finally.

Raine added Parmesan cheese and chili flakes to the table. "Same."

Keaton pulled out her chair.

Okay, Raine could get used to this. As she sat, she grinned. "Such manners."

"I try." He sat in front of the other plate. "The pizza smells delicious."

"It's from the pizzeria on First Avenue. Convenient and good. Dig in."

He took a slice of each kind. "Not sure who else you're expecting tonight."

"I got the largest size in case you had a big appetite. If not, I'll have leftovers."

"A good plan."

"Timmy's been on me about skipping meals."

"Someone should be." Keaton took a bite. "Delicious."

A little bit of cheese hung on the side of his mouth, but she wasn't sure which appeared tastier. That or his full, kissable lips.

Huh? Where had that come from?

As Raine gulped her iced tea, Keaton wiped his mouth. The cheese was gone, but those lips…

She took another sip, wishing the glass was full of ice.

"Callie mentioned you were from Seattle. Is that where your family lives?"

Raine picked up her glass and took a long sip of iced tea. She hated this question. Few knew the truth. "They did. I'm an only child. My parents are dead."

His face fell. "Oh, Raine. I'm so sorry. I shouldn't have—"

"It's fine. Okay, not fine, but it happened five years ago. I miss them, and I still cry sometimes, but it's not like it was."

"I can't imagine. My parents might annoy me at times, but—"

"I hope you never experience that kind of loss."

Keaton nodded. "Me too."

She didn't go around saying she was an orphan. The pity in her neighbors' eyes was one reason she'd wanted to get out of Seattle. The cost of living had been the other. But she recognized the curiosity in Keaton's eyes. It wasn't as if he couldn't do an internet search and find the obituaries and the news articles.

"I don't mind talking about it." Even if she didn't tell many people. Something about Keaton was different. They might be opposites in every way, but he was…kind. Stuck up and stuffy, but kind. And he'd brought dessert tonight. That had earned him bonus points. Not that she was keeping track. "I mean, I'm in Silver Falls because of what happened to them."

He angled his shoulders toward her. "What do you mean?"

"My parents never had much money. They both worked, sometimes more than one job if they had to. They believed in owning not renting and having life insurance. My dad always said if you have it you won't need it."

The sound of Dad's voice, loud and full of amusement, played in her head like one of the voice messages she still had on her cell phone. A familiar heat behind her eyelids made her glance around the eating nook with its wood-framed windows and crown molding.

"That's how I could afford to buy this house and open Tea Leaves and Coffee Beans. I always wanted my own coffee shop, but my mom never drank the stuff. She preferred tea so…"

A familiar emptiness in her chest expanded.

Oh, no. Raine didn't need the rush of grief with Keaton there. She didn't have much control, but it usually came in two different ways—rolling to shower her in a gentle wave or swamping her like a tsunami. This felt like the first, so she picked up a slice of pizza and ate, focusing all her attention on the tastes in her mouth and chewing.

After she swallowed, her eyelids no longer burned.

As soon as she set the pizza on her plate, Keaton covered her hand with his. "I thought the name of your shop was clever, but what a wonderful way to honor your parents. I had no idea the story behind it."

"Few do."

"How come?"

Another shrug. "It's not like people want to hear that your parents died in a hot air balloon outing. They'd won a package through my dad's work and invited me to go with them, but I thought..."

Her voice cracked. She wet her lips.

"It was their twenty-fifth wedding anniversary, so I told them to go without me. A special date with just the two of them."

Keaton sucked in a breath. "If you'd gone..."

"I wouldn't be here." She stared at his hand over hers. No one had touched her—not like this—in months, and she wanted to slide her fingers so his fell between hers. That would almost be like holding hands. "I...miss them."

There was nothing else she could say about how many times she picked up the phone to call them only to remember she couldn't. Or the holidays alone. That had stopped after she met Emmett, but she'd be back to celebrating those on her own in November and December.

Keaton rubbed his thumb against her hand. "I'm sure you do."

Heat pooled on her cheeks. "I usually don't tell people. Not sure what got into me."

He kept his hand on hers. She was grateful for that.

"I asked," he said in a soft tone. "You're tired. You're understaffed. There's the Boo Bash too."

She raised her gaze to meet his. "Though I have help for that last one."

Their gazes held, lingering, until Keaton looked at his plate.

"You do." He lifted his hand from hers and drank. "So, are you ready to discuss the Boo Bash?"

Yes, no, maybe. Give her a second and one of those three answers would be true.

"That's the reason I'm here," he added.

Right. But for some odd reason, that disappointed her.

Talk about being foolish. "Find anything useful in the bin?"

"The results from a survey from last year's event was eye-opening. Most parents sounded like Robin. Less candy. More activities."

Of course they did. Raine slumped in her chair. "I get it. I really do. But candy is so much easier. I don't remember if there were other activities because I was in the shop passing out candy to all the trick-or-treaters. That was chaotic enough. The thought of more sounds like…"

She gulped.

"A lot more work," Keaton finished for her.

Raine nodded and ate more pizza. A good thing she'd bought an extra-large. She needed lots of food to take her mind off this.

"The goal of the Boo Bash is…"

"For the kids to dress up and have fun. The Wednesday before Halloween is a half day at the elementary school. The event starts at one. Kids wear their costumes and go to each First Avenue Shop. Some shop owners dress up."

"Did yours?"

"We did." She expected him to ask what as, but he didn't. "The candy was provided so that was easy-peasy."

"You sound like Taryn."

"I'll take that as a compliment."

"It was meant as one."

Their gazes met. Something passed between them. Raine didn't know what. Nor was she sure she wanted to know. She stared at the half-eaten slice on her plate.

"The first time I came to Silver Falls, First Avenue had been barricaded on both ends. There was a stage set up. A choir sang. People milled about."

"That's when they name the winner of the Christmas window decorating contest. It's the biggest event of the year, so they go all out."

"I was thinking the Boo Bash could do something similar."

"Have a choir?"

"Entertainment. Games. Crafts."

Her jaw dropped. "That sounds like a lot."

"Candy would be easier."

She nodded.

"But easier isn't always better." Keaton sounded like he was trying to convince her.

It wouldn't work. "I don't have time."

"I do."

"Professor—"

"My name's Keaton."

"Fine, Keaton." Tension settled between them. She shifted in her chair but couldn't get comfortable. "I get what you're saying, but that would be a lot for a committee to take on let alone the two of us."

"I'm not talking a haunted house or hayrides."

"Is that what you had in Beverly Hills?"

"There were haunted houses in the area, but there's more to Halloween than trick-or-treating. Games, crafts, there could be a scavenger hunt or a passport where the kids get a stamp from each store and a prize at the end."

She stiffened. "A prize?"

"That's where the candy comes in, or some shops have trick-or-treating. The others do something else."

Raine didn't want to keep shooting him down, but...

"I can see how much you've thought about this. But I'll be honest. I spent what free time I had this afternoon leaving messages for applicants who were told I wasn't hiring by an ex-employee. I hired Robin and hope things will be turning around staffing wise."

He was listening to her, so she continued.

"But owning a business is like juggling double-ended knives. There is no safe side that won't cut you. I'm always waiting for the next shoe to drop. And imagining this kind of Boo Bash feels like a pair of Doc Martens just hit the top of my head."

"Too much work?"

She nodded. "I don't have it in me. Not right now."

Maybe not ever.

"I'm not trying to put more on your plate," he countered.

She gave him a look.

"This is more than putting up fliers with the event details, ordering bags of candy, and giving the bags to shops to hand out. But what if I do all the leg work?"

She stared at him in disbelief. "Why would you want to do that?"

Keaton pressed his shoulders back.

She doubted he was trying to be cute, but he was.

He raised his chin. "Andrews family members tend to throw themselves into projects one hundred and ten percent."

"Taryn must fit right in."

Keaton laughed, lightening the atmosphere. "She does."

"You have great ideas, but I'm the worst person who could get assigned the Boo Bash. I'm burnt out on events and the association itself."

"Callie mentioned you organized the Valentine's event."

No doubt his family also mentioned what Raine went through while she planned the dance. Not trusting her voice, she nodded.

"I understand." He refilled their glasses with iced tea. "Halloween isn't a big deal to me. No trick-or-treaters come to my door. I'll dress up for undergraduate classes only because some of them have never been away from home on a holiday. And I give out candy as they leave."

Okay, the man was meant to be a professor.

Or a dad.

Stop. She shouldn't be thinking about Keaton like that even if she could imagine little boys with short brown hair and glasses make-believing they were in Asgard or some other mythic locale their father told tales about. Now, she was just getting carried away.

Raine ate more pizza.

"But I have research skills," he added. "I can come up with something."

She wiped her mouth with a napkin. "I'm sure you do and can, Pro—Keaton."

He leaned toward her. "I have a proposal for you."

A good thing Raine wasn't eating or drinking anything, or she might have choked. "A what?"

"I propose two courses of action for the Boo Bash."

The least she could do was listen to him. "Go on."

"The first is a traditional Boo Bash with only trick-or-treating."

"And the second?"

"I put together ideas for a Boo Bash with activities and only some trick-or-treating."

"How long do you need?"

"We don't have that much time, so we could meet on Saturday, if you have time."

"At the coffee shop?"

"You're working?"

"Timmy is scheduled, but he can't work alone the entire time."

"The coffee shop will be fine. I'll text you when I know a time."

Her pulse kicked up a notch at the thought of seeing him again. On second thought, it must be him wanting to be so helpful. "I'll be there. Anything else?"

Keaton glanced at the bin. "It can wait."

"Help yourself to the pizza. I'm saving room for dessert. What are we having?"

"I almost bought a pumpkin spice cake with a caramel drizzle, but Jayden mentioned you were a fan of their chocolate marble cake, and they had one left so…"

It was her turn to lean forward. "Those aren't on the everyday menu, and they sell out whenever they make them."

Keaton raised the lid of the box. "You're in luck."

She stared at the chocolate icing on the layered cake. Her mouth watered. "It's my favorite."

"Then let's slice into this bad boy so you don't have to wait any longer."

Bad boy. She nearly laughed. He'd called the bin that too. If only a brainy professor was her type…

But Keaton wasn't. Raine got the feeling she wasn't his either.

At least they had cake. "I'll get a knife, forks, and plates."

Chapter Nine

FOR TWO DAYS, Keaton dove deep into researching Halloween. Not from an academic perspective but from a kid's point of view. He read articles and watched cartoons. Whatever he could find. An interesting pursuit, which he wanted to analyze and compare to his usual endeavors. But not until he finished the Boo Bash proposals. A good thing he had enough info for the second one.

He'd asked Callie, Taryn, and Margot about how much shops did for each of the events. He wanted to be mindful of the work they asked for and to not overwhelm anyone. What he discovered shouldn't have surprised him. Only three events required individual businesses to go all out: the Christmas window decorating contest, the spring shindig, and the summer fair. Which meant, if they—okay, he— wanted the Boo Bash to be more than handing out candy, everything would need to be put together and given to the businesses in an easy-to-understand package.

More work.

As Raine had mentioned.

But the idea of work wouldn't scare him off.

On Friday morning at Margot's dining room table, he

scribbled in his notebook.

Call him old-school, but he preferred pen and paper.

The only issue…

Whenever he thought about Halloween, Raine came to mind. The two had become entwined in Keaton's mind. He kept wanting to text about the ghoulish games he'd discovered. Except she didn't have time for that.

For him.

Saturday would be there soon enough.

He wanted to make life easier for Raine. Her story replayed in his mind.

What happened to her parents broke his heart. Touching her hand hadn't been enough but he hadn't dared more. Anything else would have been…inappropriate. More unlike him than ordering a different coffee.

He couldn't and didn't want to imagine what she must have gone through. Sure, his siblings teased each other, but he loved them. No matter how hard Mom and Dad pushed, to suddenly have them gone from his life…

He shuddered.

Raine had superhero powers to survive what happened. His respect for her kept growing. And when her smile lit up her face…

"Working hard, I see."

Keaton dropped his pen. Margot stood in the living room. She was smiling as usual. "I didn't realize you were working a half day."

"I'm not. I forgot my lunch." She studied the table. "Why aren't you working at the coffee shop?"

"I'm watching videos and forgot to pack my headphones. I'm not a fan of AirPods. I keep losing them."

"Have you eaten?"

If Margot didn't have the quilt shop, she would have made a wonderful café owner or B&B host. She loved to take care of people, but Keaton wouldn't make more work for her. "I had a late breakfast."

"I'll grab my lunch and be off." She eyed the paperwork on the table. "Is that for the Boo Bash?"

"Doing some research for Raine."

Margot's face lit up. "Knew you were the right man for her."

Wait. What? Every muscle tensed. Keaton's gaze shot to hers. "Excuse me?"

"To help. With the Boo Bash."

His stiff neck relaxed. He'd been warned about Margot's matchmaking. Not that he and Raine were compatible. They were opposites. If he taught a STEM subject, he would come up with a magnet analogy, but alas he didn't. Though if he said *alas* in a conversation his family would rib him, even though it was only four letters and they all used ten-dollar words.

"There's that smile I love." Margot winked. "You should use it on the lovely singletons in town."

"You're incorrigible."

"I am." She wagged her finger. "But wait and see. Big-city men always fall for someone from a small town."

Must be something in the water.

Or a certain quilt shop owner.

Keaton was smart enough not to say that aloud. "Enjoy your lunch."

She rolled her eyes and headed into the kitchen. A moment later, the back door slammed shut.

He returned to his list. Some ideas were outrageous, but in the brainstorming phase, he would cross off nothing.

His cell phone buzzed with three text notifications.

He glanced at the screen. It was a message from Lilia, Dean Fredricks's assistant.

> **Lilia:** Hope you're doing well. I miss seeing photos of Rex. I don't know if you were notified but a visiting professor position opened in Cambridge.

Keaton's pulse skyrocketed. Was this real or had he daydreamed the perfect position? He reread the message. "Cambridge."

He pumped his fist and kept reading.

> **Lilia:** Boston would be a good fit. You'd be perfect for the position with your qualifications. I sent an email with more information. Texting to make sure you open that.

Applying for jobs meant staying on top of his email. No one from the university had been in touch with him. Thank goodness for Lilia.

Keaton opened the email and clicked the link. He read the job listing. Each word made his heart swell.

"I'm more than qualified."

But he'd been qualified at his old university too.

"Can't take things for granted."

He kept reading. The position started in January. That

meant he could spend the holidays in Silver Falls before moving east. He pushed aside the Boo Bash stuff. He filled out the application. He'd become an expert at applications. Something two weeks ago, he wouldn't have claimed. As soon as he finished, he reread the application. Satisfied, he uploaded his CV and hit submit.

Done.

He picked up his phone and typed a reply to Lilia.

Me: *Thank you. I hadn't heard about the position. I've applied. Here are the newest pics of Rex. Thanks again. And I hope the first day of the quarter goes well.*

Keaton still couldn't believe someone else was teaching his class. Nothing he could do about that except look for a new job like this one.

He hit *send*.

Relief washed over him. All he had to do was wait to hear if his application made the first cut. He hoped it did because this was exactly the kind of position he wanted to find. Temporary, yes, but he was confident this would lead to something better...bigger.

That buoyed his spirits.

Time to take a break. A walk to stretch his muscles would be good and a celebratory drink at the coffee shop. What more could he ask for?

THIRTY MINUTES LATER, Keaton stood in line at the coffee shop. As Robin took orders, Raine prepared the drinks. Two people stood in line ahead of him. He didn't mind the wait, especially when training a new employee would help Raine in the future.

When it was his turn, he stepped to the corner.

Robin beamed. "Welcome to Tea Leaves and Coffee Beans. What can I get for you today?"

"Your boss is introducing me to the joy of pumpkin spice."

Raine glanced over at him. "Keaton's coffees are on the house. His reward for helping me with the Boo Bash. I'll take care of him."

"Sure thing." Robin's smile widened. "Is this to go?"

He hadn't planned on staying, but why not? "For here."

"Someone will bring over your beverage shortly."

"Thanks." Raine was busy making drinks, so he didn't say anything to her. No way would he be a burden or a distraction to her when she had so much work.

He sat at his usual corner table with a nearby plug in case his computer's battery ran out of juice. Not that he'd brought the laptop today. He'd left it and the Boo Bash stuff on Margot's dining room table to return to later.

Someone set a cup on his table. "It's a Pumpkin Spice Double Shot on Ice."

He recognized Raine's voice. She stood next to him.

Keaton picked up the cup. "Pulling out all the stops today to make sure I don't fall asleep tonight."

Her closed-mouth smile was too mischievous to be compared to Mona Lisa's. "Customer service at its finest."

"Such modesty."

"You're one to talk." She sounded amused.

He deserved that. "You've got me. Callie's the only one who got that gene in our family, but I'm not as bad as my brothers or parents."

Keaton's joke fell flat, but he didn't think Raine noticed. He'd been the same or worse than Mom, Dad, Flynn, and Garrett. Losing his job made Keaton see himself differently. His world, too.

He'd grown up with wealthy, successful parents, who paid for his education without blinking an eye. He'd had zero student loans and as much financial help as he wanted. Success was assumed and expected from a young age. But there'd been parental support for as long as he'd known it existed. Add in growing up in Beverly Hills...

The definition of privilege.

The university had been one more bubble world where he'd been a guppy but had zero doubt he'd grow into a koi.

But he no longer felt invincible. His certainty in his plans and himself had been shaken to the core. He'd believed everything he wanted would happen. Now, not so much.

"You've only been in town for five days. I'll need a few more data points," Raine teased. "Robin has to leave, so I need to get back."

"Are you working alone for the rest of the day?"

"Timmy will be here in an hour." The lines on Raine's forehead returned, and Keaton wanted them to disappear somehow. "Do you need me for something?"

"Yes." The word slipped out. Keaton fought the urge to grimace. "I mean, no. It can wait. Until you have more time."

"Okay." She returned to the counter.

What was wrong with him?

He removed his glasses and rubbed his eyes. At least he'd have time to think of what to ask Raine other than his original question—if she wanted to get together before this weekend.

That hadn't been in reference to the Boo Bash. Keaton wasn't ready to present his proposals. He had wanted to make her feel better. A night out where she could forget about the coffee shop and the Boo Bash would do the trick.

But Keaton couldn't.

Untrue.

He could, but he shouldn't.

Raine was his opposite in many ways. He was supposed to be helping her with the event, not trying to get her to relax and have fun and spend more time with him.

Yet, a part of him still wanted that. He just had no idea why.

RAINE MADE KEATON a different pumpkin spice drink. One without two espresso shots that would keep him awake all night. She swirled whipped cream on top and stuck in a straw. This drink was more of a dessert, but a few calories shouldn't matter. "I'm going to deliver this."

"Take a break while you're there." Timmy worked on an iced latte. "There's no line, and you might not get another chance until later."

"Sometimes I wonder who's the boss around here."

He pointed to himself before going back to work.

Raine made her way to Keaton, who stared at his phone. As she approached, he didn't look up. She set his cup close to him and took out her phone from her pocket. "Must be something interesting."

Keaton glanced up, smiled, and placed his phone face down on the table. "Catching up with our family chat."

"Callie mentioned your video calls."

He laughed. "They used to be our way to keep in touch with Callie. Now three of us are in Silver Falls."

"Mind company?"

"Sit."

Raine did.

He took a sip of his new drink. "Pumpkin spice milkshake?"

"We also call them frappes. Can't use the 'uccino' ending because it's trademarked." She had to give kudos to the marketing department at the biggest coffee shop franchise in the world. "But customers do."

He brought the straw to his mouth.

Hers went dry.

Anticipation. That was what it was.

Keaton's face brightened. "I liked the others, but this is my favorite so far."

Yes! She straightened. "There are more for you to try."

"Can't wait."

Neither could she. He hadn't brought his laptop bag with him. "Not working on your book today?"

"No. I'm celebrating."

"What's the occasion?"

"I submitted a job application for a position. I hope I get it."

"You're leaving the university where you teach?"

His posture went ramrod stiff. His face flushed.

"I, um…" Keaton took a sip of his drink and grimaced as if he'd gotten a brain freeze. "I lost my job a couple of weeks ago. Budget cuts wiped out my department."

No wonder he'd shown up unexpectedly in Silver Falls. "That sucks."

He laughed. "It does. I came to Silver Falls to regroup and figure out what to do next. My apartment was owned by the university, so it was either come here or move into my childhood bedroom at my parents'."

"Well, I'm happy you're here, and that the Boo Bash figured into your plans."

"Me, too." Keaton hoped she heard how much he meant it.

"Margot must've thought you needed something else to do like the Boo Bash—like applying for jobs and working on your book aren't full-time jobs on their own.

"I can only spend so much time on each. She wanted to help you, too."

"As long as it's with the Boo Bash and not…"

"Matchmaking," they said in unison.

Both laughed.

Then, her expression grew more serious. She leaned forward. "I'm glad you came to Silver Falls. I hope that job works out for you, but my mom always told me when one door closes, another opens. Only she believed in slamming the door fast, so the bugs didn't fly inside."

The deep, rich sound of Keaton's laughter wrapped around Raine like one of Margot's quilts.

She glanced at the counter. A line was forming. "I should get back."

He picked up his cup. "I'm taking this with me for the walk home. It'll put me in the right mood to work."

"On your book?"

"Maybe later. I have two proposals to finish up so I can present them to you tomorrow."

"Thanks for taking the Boo Bash so seriously."

"It's important." He sounded so earnest, as if the community event had an impact beyond one small town.

But earnest wasn't the same as excited, the way he got when he talked about writing. "Your book is important too so don't push it aside."

He blinked. "You are the only one besides my mom who thinks so."

"You light up whenever you mention it. That tells me your book is important to you." She winked. "You're not the only one who reads body language."

"Well-done." His gaze locked on hers.

Her breath stilled. The noises in the shop faded.

"See you tomorrow," he said, breaking whatever spell was between them.

"Looking forward to it." As in seeing him, not hearing about the Boo Bash.

She swallowed. What in the world was happening?

Chapter Ten

SATURDAY MORNING DRAGGED. Raine kept busy, hoping the afternoon would arrive sooner than later. She wanted to hear what Keaton had come up with. Timmy took his lunch break first, and then it was her turn. But anticipation kept her on edge.

When the bell jingled, Raine glanced at the door. Pippa walked in.

Not Keaton.

Raine slumped. She'd thought he would be there by now.

"If I had a dollar for every time you've glanced at the door, I would have more money than what's in the tip jar." Timmy prepared a caramel hot apple cider. "What's going on?"

"Just waiting for Keaton. We're discussing plans for the Boo Bash."

Timmy snickered. "Only the Boo Bash?"

"Yes." The word rushed out faster than the steam on the coffee machine.

His smile suggested he didn't believe her. "If you say so, Boss."

The bell on the door jingled yet again.

Don't look.

Raine couldn't stop herself, and she was happy for the lack of self-control.

Keaton entered, wearing a pair of khakis and a long-sleeved navy shirt. His laptop bag's strap hung on his shoulder. He headed to the counter with purposeful steps.

Raine straightened her apron streaked with stains after an incident with foamed milk. Too late to change into a clean one. She went to the cash register to take his order.

"Hey." Raine hoped her smile was cheery not manic. Her hand hovered over the cash register from habit until she remembered his drink was on the house. She lowered her hand to her side. "Ready to try something new?"

"I was debating whether to go have an Americano or keep switching it up."

She shook off the disappointment. One cup of coffee didn't matter. Well, to anyone else but her. "Your choice."

The two words tasted like used coffee grinds in her mouth.

He read the menu. "Decisions, decisions."

Raine said nothing. She had a feeling "don't go back into your standard cup" wouldn't go over well.

"I'll take another pumpkin spice," Keaton said finally. "Your choice of drinks."

Yes! Raine didn't pump her fist, but she wiggled her toes. "I know what I'll be making you."

"I'll grab a table. Come over when you have time."

She didn't look at the menu to pick his next drink. She

blended pumpkin, milk, and spices. Next, she steamed the mixture before adding espresso shots, a single layer of milk and a sprinkle of spices on top.

Robin came out from the back. "Everything's put away."

"Great. I'll be with Keaton. Wave if you need me."

Raine carried over the drink. It wasn't until she was halfway to the table when she realized she hadn't let Robin reply.

Impatient much?

Raine glanced over her shoulder.

A grinning Robin shooed Raine away.

With hot cheeks, Raine set the drink on Keaton's table. "This is my take on a pumpkin spice flat white."

"The name sounds fancy."

"Try it," she urged.

Keaton blew on the coffee. His lips puckered.

Was that how he looked before he kissed someone? She swallowed.

He tasted it. "Oh, this is a little thicker. Richer. I like it. Thanks."

A thrill shot through her. "Glad you like it."

"Ready to Boo Bash with me?"

"I am." Raine sat and leaned back. "What do you have for me?"

He lifted the top page off the closest stack of papers. It was a flyer with Halloween clipart and the words "A Trick-or-Treating Event" in bold letters. The date and time were in a smaller but readable font.

"The first is a traditional Boo Bash. I made up the flyer

based on the ones I found in the bin. A checklist had where to hang them around town: businesses, the library bulletin board, schools."

"Looks great." And one less thing for her to have to do.

"The place where the town orders from offers other items." He opened a catalog with sticky notes on various pages to show her spider rings, vampire teeth and Halloween-themed pencils. "It'll be tight with the budget but it's doable. There won't be money for anything else."

He impressed her. It must have taken him time to figure out what items they could afford. "I appreciate you researching candy alternatives and keeping the workload down."

"Proposal one is the easiest. It's also the most boring."

"You make that sound like a bad thing. I like the other items you found. Those aren't boring."

His eye twitched.

She hadn't seen that before.

"The second proposal will take more work and volunteers but… Let me show you." He turned over the top page on the other stack to a different flyer.

This flyer didn't mention trick-or-treating. Instead, it listed more—crafts and other activities.

Raine peered closer. "The First Avenue Halloween Scavenger Hunt."

He nodded. His excitement was palpable. "The street would have to be closed like they do in December."

"I'm sure city hall or the police department have a form to do that. I can see what's required if we go this route." She emphasized the last part of the sentence.

"Or I can," he offered.

She wanted to take him up on it, but common sense prevailed. "I'm local and in charge of the event. It might go over well coming from someone putting on an event for the association."

He nodded. "I spoke to Taryn. She's willing to supervise kids decorating a sugar cookie. Taryn can do pumpkins and bats. Mr. Jones can get small pumpkins the kids can color with markers and stickers. And Margot can sew scarecrows the kids can stuff with straw in front of the town hall. For your shop, you can hand out small cups of Witches' Brew or pumpkin punch instead of candy."

Okay, she was impressed times ten with this proposal. He'd even been proactive by finding help for activities ahead of time. But she had no idea what was involved with the scavenger hunt. She scanned the various pages under the second flyer.

He'd listened to her. Raine wanted to hug Keaton. She studied his plans. Every activity was detailed with cost estimates and the number of volunteers required.

"You're right," she admitted. "This one would be more fun."

"You'd be surprised what you can discover on the internet. Especially Pinterest."

"You succeeded pulling it all together. I would have never considered any of this."

"In full transparency, my first effort was, shall we say, too highbrow for kids. My second included glitter, which I learned is a '*no*' for parents."

That made her laugh. "No glitter experience, so I'll take your word for it."

"Research." His cheeks reddened. He quickly opened a notebook. "Here are plans for a haunted house, corn maze, and a DJ playing Halloween music, but those things depend on the budget and volunteers. The two of us can only do so much."

"After hearing proposal number two, number one sounds boring."

His face lit up with an I-told-you-so expression. "That's why I saved the second proposal for last. What do you think?"

Each word dripped with anticipation—thick like the caramel apples were dipped into.

"The scavenger hunt for stamps, stickers, and items are more interesting than getting candy. The crafts and activities give the event a good mix so it's not all the same."

His mouth dropped open. "You're considering it?"

"Yes, but we may have to simplify your plans. I want to make sure we can pull it off successfully."

"Of course."

"Kids will love it. We could simplify things if we needed to. Could you leave the stuff with me?" She glanced at Raine and Timmy, both with big smiles, watching from behind the counter. They were as bad as Margot. Okay, not really, but Raine needed to stop them from thinking anything was going on. "I promise to review it later, and we can meet tomorrow afternoon to discuss it. Around four? My house?"

Keaton grinned wider than any jack-o'-lantern. The way

he stared at her made Raine feel like the only woman in his world. "Sounds great."

Yes, it did. She smiled.

"It's a date." Raine realized what she'd said. "A Boo Bash date."

Somehow, that sounded worse. She fought the urge to cringe.

Ugh. If only she could rewind time and try again. But all she could do was smile and ignore the wicked laughter in Keaton's eyes.

SUNDAY AFTERNOON, KEATON settled back on Raine's peacock-blue couch. The color was bright and made a statement, yet it fit the character of the older single-story house. He hadn't seen beyond her living room, kitchen, and bathroom, but her house was cozy and comfortable.

Welcoming.

Still, Keaton fidgeted. Raine wanting to simplify his plans brought his final meeting with Dean Fredricks to mind. Simplify wasn't the same as the university's budget cuts, but the word brought the same emotions and nerves. He had no idea why he was so invested in the Boo Bash or Raine's opinion.

"I'm almost finished in here," Raine called from the kitchen. "A pot of coffee is brewing, and my vanilla tea is steeping."

The tea smelled delicious, but he preferred coffee, when working.

"No rush. We're making good progress."

And they were.

Keaton hadn't realized how easy working with Raine would be. Her project manager skills were top notch. She listened and asked questions and never dismissed an idea outright, even though in hindsight—his, not hers—she probably should have. She respected his work and him. Which meant volunteering for the Boo Bash wasn't only busy work but fun, too.

Focus on the fun.

He blew out a breath and stretched his legs in front of him.

With the edited Halloween scavenger hunt checklist on his lap to reread, he stretched out his feet.

Raine carried two cups into the living room. She wore faded jeans, a cropped sweater, and mismatched purple and green fuzzy socks that made Keaton smile each time he noticed them. She set the drinks on the table next to the papers and their cell phones. "Caffeine to keep us going."

She sat at the other end of the couch.

His only complaint about the sofa?

Too wide.

A cushion separated him and Raine. If she had a love seat, they would be sitting closer.

Not a date.

He glanced at the plate with two scones. "Sorry I ate the other scones on the walk here. They're addictive."

"They are, and it was sweet of Taryn to send them with you."

Keaton sipped his coffee. As delicious as a drink from her shop.

She picked up a piece of paper. "I went over the activities. They're great, but we need to cut a few." Her tone was soft, almost sympathetic.

His stomach clenched even though he knew this was coming. "I get it. We don't have enough volunteers."

"Or budget."

Keaton knew that one too well. His job loss had been a numbers game. "It always comes down to money."

He'd offered to pay Margot rent, but she'd acted offended and said no. Instead, he did chores and ran errands for her. This morning, he'd replaced all the smoke detector batteries. And no dirty dishes remained in the sink for long. Not on his watch.

"Money and time."

Their gazes locked. The connection he'd felt with her roared back to life. It wasn't always there, but something flowed between them. Stronger now. "There's never enough time."

Maybe for her, but time was all he had right now. Raine, however, wasn't talking about his situation. She meant the Boo Bash.

"Before we move on, let's finalize the scavenger hunt." Keaton lifted the list off his lap. He'd used a red pen to cross out items that would be too complicated for a community event and scribbled in simpler ones. "Our revised list looks good to me. What do you think?"

Raine took the page and then grinned. "This one is

done."

Her enthusiastic voice made him smile. "I'll make corrections to the file. On to the activity list?"

That was what she wanted to simplify.

Nodding, she reached for another piece of paper. "I love the idea of decorating mini pumpkins with markers and stickers, but I think the cookie decorating is enough. It's cheaper and easier for them to carry around in their treat bags or eat right there."

"That works for me."

As Raine studied the list, she rubbed her chin. "Coloring's a good activity, but what if we took it a step further?"

"I thought you wanted to simplify?"

"I do, but I had an idea for a card-making station."

"Halloween cards?"

Raine nodded. "There are five days between the Boo Bash and Halloween. Instead of taking their cards home, we ask the kids to write a note to a resident at the local assisted living center, and we can deliver them before the thirty-first."

"No pumpkins to carry and a community service project." He thought about it. "You're brilliant."

"Thanks. I'm more street smart and common sense than book smart like you, but I like the sound of brilliant."

"I like the card idea." Truth was, Keaton liked Raine.

"I'm impressed with all your mock-ups."

His chest puffed. "Margot helped me. I'm not crafty."

"Could've fooled me."

He shrugged. "But now I see why people enjoy teaching kindergarten and first grade. The crafts are cool."

"Art projects are fun, but they can be messy."

"Hence the no glitter rule."

"No one wants First Avenue coated in sparkly stuff." She kept staring at Keaton, but he didn't know why.

Maybe it was time to ask. "What's going on?"

"What do you mean?"

"You keep looking at me?"

"I'm just…happy."

That didn't tell Keaton much. He leaned toward her, wanting to know what she was thinking and how he fit into it. "Because of the Boo Bash?"

Nodding, Raine motioned to the coffee table. "Working together has made things so much easier than I thought it would be. The Boo Bash is coming together faster than I expected. Robin's working out better than I could imagine, and I hired a guy named Parker, who has experience. Everything's turned around since you offered to help me. Now if I could just find one or two more baristas." Raine held up her hands. "Oh, I didn't mean you."

Her tone was serious. Too serious. That was his fault. "You claimed you wanted to hire me."

"Yes, but it's not the kind of job you want."

She may have forgiven him, but she hadn't forgotten. "It isn't, but I didn't know I'd be organizing the Boo Bash with you and enjoying myself so much. I might like being a barista, too."

"Or you may not have set a high bar for your enjoyment level and you're being a nice guy about it."

"No!" He covered his chest with his hand and slumped

as if shot. "Nice is a four-letter word when you're a man. Everybody claims they want to date a nice guy, but no one does."

"Well, I like nice. Not that we're dating."

The way the second sentence rushed out was cute.

He grinned. "I suppose nice isn't the worst thing someone could say about me."

"Oh, there are much worse. Just ask your sister."

Keaton laughed. "Very funny. And correct."

Raine drank. Her cell phone buzzed.

"Emmett" flashed on the screen.

Wait. Wasn't that Raine's ex?

She stared at the phone with her mouth forming a perfect o.

Keaton couldn't tell if she was shocked or happy. "Need to reply to that?"

Her gaze jerked to meet his.

Another text notification sounded.

He kept his eyes on her.

She swallowed. "I've never made him wait for a reply."

"Go ahead."

"No." She squared her shoulders. "That door's closed."

Interesting choice of words given what she'd told him her mom used to say. "Does that mean you're ready to open another one?"

Raine dragged her upper teeth over her lower lip. "Is that how it works?"

"In some cases, but there's not only one way."

"Good." She took a sip of coffee. "Because I'm not ready

for another relationship. It was hard finding out Emmett wanted a different life than the one I imagined we'd share after four years together. We tried long distance twice until he broke up with me in April. I haven't dated since then. And to be honest, I'm not even sure what to do if I wanted to open the door."

Keaton appreciated her openness. And he got an idea. It might not be one of his better ones, but… "I can help you."

Her eyebrows squished together. "You're helping with the Boo Bash."

Her confused expression was cute, but he got why she didn't understand. Sometimes he was two steps ahead of people. At least according to his mom, who suggested he slow down and not assume everyone's mind worked like his. "I meant to help you open another door."

Fear flashed in her eyes. "Like a date?"

No, she wasn't ready for that. "More like a practice one."

"Practice." She spoke slowly as if she were testing out the word. "A practice date with a professor?"

That did sound a bit out there. He shrugged. "Unless it's too soon."

She shook her head. "I don't want Emmett back. But I'm not ready for another door to be open."

"But when it does…" If the men around Silver Falls were smart, she wouldn't be single for long.

Her mouth quirked. "I suppose practice wouldn't hurt. But I don't have much time…"

Raine didn't, but he had a sweet idea that might appeal to her. "What if we go for dessert? The bakery's patio is still open."

"Dessert." She tapped her chin. "If I remember back to dating one-oh-one, dessert's a step up from having coffee. It's for when you're trying to decide if you want to get to know someone better."

"Yes. And you're not committed for a significant amount of time that leaves you regretting all your life choices over four or five courses."

"Maybe not life choices." Raine laughed. "But an evening's choice for sure."

"So, what do you say?"

"I could be up for dessert at Lawson's. I love that place."

"Most people in Silver Falls love the place. Would tomorrow night work?"

"As long as it's after the coffee shop closes."

Keaton knew she worked a lot, but seven days a week was too much. He hoped the new barista worked out. "It's a date."

She nodded. "A practice date."

"Looking forward to it." And he was.

Raine held up her list. "We have a couple more activities on the Boo Bash to discuss."

Right. The Boo Bash. Keaton had forgotten the reason he was there. All he wanted was to go to Lawson's. Dating wasn't a subject he thought he'd be tutoring on, but he couldn't wait for a practice date with Raine.

Chapter Eleven

DON'T BE NERVOUS.

Monday evening, Raine parked in front of Lawson's Bakery. If this was a real date, she wouldn't be driving herself. Except it wasn't.

She glanced in the rearview mirror. She couldn't see much other than eyeshadow and mascara. Not that she needed to wear makeup for a practice date.

Pathetic.

Raine smoothed her hair.

Who admitted they weren't sure about dating or that they didn't know how to date? Even if it were the truth.

Again, pathetic.

She had no idea how to date without being in a relationship. Not that she'd had many—a grand total of three if she counted Scott in high school. None had followed the meet, go out a few times to get to know each other, and then decide to be exclusive. Emmett and she had never had an official date until weeks after they'd become boyfriend and girlfriend.

Not that she was complaining. It had been perfect.

No angst over whether they'd call. No overanalyzing every moment they were together. No wondering if they were friends or more than friends or something in between.

Was fear keeping her from wanting to date?

No answer came.

She got out of the car with her purse, shut the door, and pressed the lock on the key fob. She placed the purse strap over her shoulder. Keaton wasn't waiting outside so she went into the bakery.

The interior was light and bright, social media perfect after Garrett had painted the walls and replaced the furniture and fixtures as a surprise for Taryn. That was right before he told her he would be working remotely for his law firm and proposed.

Brecken, dressed in white with a black apron, waved from behind the counter. "You're in luck. Me and Carl are here tonight. You know what that means."

"Extra whipped cream?"

"You know it." Brecken tilted his head. "Though you'd need to order something with whipped cream. Then again most desserts taste good with it."

"I'll keep that in mind." Raine glanced at the daily specials board. Unfortunately, marble cake wasn't listed. But two other items caught her eye.

"Sorry I'm late," Keaton said from behind her. He came up to her side. "I was on our weekly family video call and lost track of the time."

"Absent-minded professor?"

"Only occasionally. We were debating where to spend Thanksgiving."

Must be nice to have those conversations. She focused on

the menu board. "Did you decide where?"

"No, but my parents and Flynn are pulling for L.A. since we'll be in Silver Falls for Christmas. They've invited Margot, Brandt's parents, and Taryn's."

Sounds like a good plan for the Andrews family. The only holiday Raine wanted to focus on was Halloween. Then, she wouldn't think about another until the Fourth of July. "Know what you want?"

"Pie sounds good."

"I'm getting the hummingbird cake."

That was another item not on the daily menu. Ever since Taryn took over running the bakery in August, she'd changed things up. Not huge changes to upset long-time customers, but specials and new items to keep things from seeming staid.

Raine headed to the counter.

Keaton touched her arm. "This was my idea, so on me."

She remembered about his job. Plus, he was helping her. She reached for her purse. "But—"

"I'm helping you with the Boo Bash and I'm unemployed, but I've got this."

"Did my body language give away what I was thinking again?"

"A little." His tone was sly. "But I'm getting to know you."

Raine drew back. "How so? You haven't been in town long."

"A week last night, but I didn't go to the coffee shop until Monday." He wagged his eyebrows. "I'm that good."

She laughed. "Participants in a practice date implies going Dutch."

"Humor me."

"This time." Raine nearly cringed at what her words suggested. "Though let's hope I don't need a second practice date."

"So far you're ahead of the curve."

"Do this a lot?"

"No, but I've been on a few dates in my time. You haven't pulled out your phone once. That earns you extra credit."

"I'd love an A."

"You're on your way."

Raine stood taller. She wanted to pass this practice date with an A+. She stepped aside so he could order.

After Brecken rang up their orders and Keaton paid, they went outside to the patio. Surprisingly, no one else was there. Instrumental music played from speakers hidden with plants. No flower baskets this time of year, but the globe light strands strung along the pergola and fairy lights on trellises gave off a soft, romantic glow. More wooden signs painted with dessert names had been added since the patio opened in July. Portable heaters kept the patio comfortable, especially now that the cooler temperatures of October had arrived.

Raine sat at a table for two.

Keaton took the seat across from her. "I wonder how long they'll keep the patio open."

"Until it starts raining too hard or if snow comes early."

"The heaters will help now that autumn's here."

She nodded. "They're nice tonight."

"Would you rather sit inside?" Keaton asked.

"This is perfect." Especially the privacy. Even though she'd lived in Silver Falls for four years, she still wasn't used to the gossip and rumors that fueled the busybodies in town. "Though Garrett did an excellent job on the interior."

"He went all out on that grand gesture and set the bar so high. Not sure anyone will be able to top that."

His serious tone matched the hard set of his jaw. He almost sounded put out.

"It's not a competition," she said.

"My family competes with everything."

"Not Callie. At least not until the Christmas window contest."

"She's an anomaly. Remember what I talked about with her not getting the same DNA as the rest of us? But it's a good thing. She makes sure the rest of us don't hurt each other."

"Taryn's lucky to have found a family like yours. She's super competitive with her Christmas windows and Summer Fair booths."

He nodded. "She fits right in with the rest of us."

Taryn had her parents, but she was an only child like Raine. Now she had in-laws and Margot thanks to Brandt's marriage to Callie.

Someday I'll have a family again.

Raine thought she'd found a new family with Emmett and his big extended family. But that wasn't meant to be. None of the Wilsons even came into the coffee shop anymore. She fiddled with her napkin.

"How's Robin working out?" Keaton asked.

"Great. I have interviews set up with a few others this coming week."

"I'm happy for you." He sounded sincere. "You need more time off."

"I do, but I'm getting there." Saying that brought a tsunami of relief.

The bakery door opened. Brecken carried out a tray and placed the contents on the table. "Hummingbird cake and water for Raine and a slice of marionberry pie a la mode and water for Keaton. If you need anything else, just wave one of us down. Enjoy the sweets."

"What do you think so far?" Keaton asked.

She hadn't taken a bite yet. She picked up her fork. "The cake looks delicious."

"I meant our date. Regretting the evening's choice?"

Raine laughed and took a bite of cake. "Not yet, but this is only a practice date. I haven't done anything embarrassing yet. So far the company's pleasant, but the evening's still young."

It was his turn to laugh. "You're doing great. Though I might have to deduct a few points from your score because the company is stellar."

Raine ate more cake. It melted in her mouth. "Well, the company did buy me this delicious dessert."

He leaned over the table with his napkin in hand. "You have a little icing on your lip."

Forget the icing.

If he moved a little closer, he could kiss her, or she could kiss him. Or they could kiss each other.

Whoa. What was she thinking?

This wasn't a real date. She needed to get those thoughts right out of her head.

He wiped her mouth with his napkin. "All gone."

She couldn't meet his eyes. Instead, she focused on her plate of cake as if tomorrow night's winning lottery numbers were about to be announced.

It wasn't Keaton, but Raine. Her attraction for him kept growing. That was a problem given dating wasn't part of her plans nor his. He would be leaving town once he found a job.

A warning bell sounded in her head.

She shoved another forkful of cake into her mouth. The sweet, melt-in-her-mouth goodness didn't stop the wild thoughts racing through her brain.

Keaton set down his fork. "If you're worried, don't be. You're doing great. I wouldn't have guessed you're not comfortable dating."

That was part of the problem. Raine was comfortable with him. No, comfortable wasn't the right word given how on-edge she felt around Keaton. But she wasn't afraid. "Thanks. You make it easy."

"You'll be ready when the door opens."

"Hope so."

She enjoyed having someone in her life. Oh, she had friends, but they also had their own lives and loves now. And she would love to have kids at some point. And she knew enough about dating to not mention the future or family or kids.

"I hope it doesn't take too long for that to open. Dating isn't part of my plans right now, but I'll leave the door ajar."

He held his scoop of pie in midair. "You've come far since yesterday."

"You're a good teacher." She scooped up more cake. "Besides, I'm over thirty, own my own business, and have only myself to rely upon. If I can't handle a practice date, then there's a problem."

"So does that mean you're ready to let me get to know you better?"

Raine scooted forward. "What do you want to know?"

KEATON HADN'T LAUGHED so much in… He couldn't remember the last time. Raine told him one story after another about incidents that happened at the various coffee shops that she'd worked at over the years. "What you're saying is Silver Falls is relatively normal compared to Seattle?"

"When it comes to funny customer stories, yes. But this town has its own quirks."

"Like a resident matchmaker?"

"Be careful, or she'll have you married off before you leave town."

Only a few crumbs remained on their plates. "I'm not interested in a relationship. Not when my life is so in flux."

"I told Margot something similar. The question is if she

listens."

"No one is forced to play along. Though I don't hear Callie or Garrett complaining."

"Callie wasn't happy about it before she fell for Brandt. Now, she's thrilled how everything turned out."

"Hey." Brecken approached them. He carried an empty tray at his side. "Hate to kick you out, but it's closing time."

"Oh." Raine folded her napkin and placed it on the table. "I had no idea it had gotten so late."

"Me, either." Keaton hadn't glanced at his phone once. "Sorry to keep you."

"No worries." Brecken grinned. "We still have to clean and prep for tomorrow, but Taryn prefers customers to be gone by then even from the patio. She's a good boss, but a stickler for rules."

Keaton laughed. "That's exactly what Garrett needs."

"Ready to go?" Raine asked.

No. He wasn't ready for the evening to end, but he didn't want Brecken and Carl to get in trouble. "Yes."

Keaton stood, pulled out a five-dollar bill from his wallet, and tossed it on the table.

"Thanks, dude." Brecken cleared the table.

Raine headed toward the rear door, and Keaton followed her into the bakery.

Behind the counter, Carl cleaned the display cabinet. "Thanks for coming in. Have a good evening."

She waved. "Everything was delicious."

"Loved the pie." Keaton opened the front door for Raine. "After you."

"Thanks."

Outside, the temperature was ten or twenty degrees colder than on the patio with the heaters nearby. Raine wore a sweater, but it wasn't that thick.

"Cold?" he asked.

"No."

A streetlamp illuminated the sidewalk. The light cast shadows on them.

She glanced through the bakery's front window. "I can't believe we closed down the bakery."

"Practice date for the win."

Raine laughed.

"They do close earlier on weekdays." A *closed* sign hung on the door. "But I can't believe Brecken kicked us out. I'll make him work extra hard during our next tutoring session for that."

"He was just doing his job."

"Don't worry, I'll go easy on Timmy."

"Thank you. I don't know what I'd do without him."

A part of Keaton wished she'd say the same thing about him. Maybe by the time the Boo Bash was over she would. He rocked back on his heels. "So how do you think it went?"

"If it means dessert and getting to know each other, then well. We know each other's favorite colors, food, TV shows, books, and movies."

"If we put everything that we discussed into a Venn diagram there wouldn't be much overlap."

"Except for food," they said in unison.

"The practice date was a success. How did I do?" she

asked.

"A-plus."

Raine did a shuffle step as if dancing. "Yay!"

"You did great." More than once he'd forgotten they weren't on a real date. "When the door opens, you'll be ready."

"You made it easy."

His chest puffed out. He couldn't help it. "You're a great date. I've gone out at times and wondered why my date said yes when all she did was stay on her phone the entire time."

"That's how Emmett and I had gotten toward the end, but the first few dates are the honeymoon time. A phone can't compete with that."

"Unless it's not meant to be."

She nodded. "It's getting late."

"You have to be at the coffee shop early."

Raine nodded. "Thanks for dessert."

"I had a great time." Dates usually ended with a kiss, but this was just for practice. He doubted suggesting a practice kiss would go over well.

"Me, too." She shifted her weight between her feet. "I'm glad you suggested doing this."

"Me, too."

Keaton wanted to ask her out again. That was how much he'd enjoyed himself. But she didn't want to date, and he was leaving town—soon, he hoped.

"We might have to come for dessert again. To celebrate our work on the Boo Bash."

"There's going to be a lot of it."

"Teamwork will get it done."

"You sound more like a coach than a professor."

"I assign group projects."

"The bane of students everywhere. Timmy always got stuck with classmates who didn't want to do any work."

"That happens sometimes, but it's a good lesson in adulting."

"Recently experienced that with a former employee."

She must be talking about the barista who got fired. "If this was a real date, I'd kiss you good night. But since this is only for practice…" He kissed her forehead. "Did you walk?"

"Drove. The hatchback right in front of us. You?"

"Walked."

"Want a ride to Margot's?"

He shoved his fingers in his pockets. "I'm good. Good night."

"See you around."

Tomorrow. Keaton planned on working at her coffee shop. He couldn't wait to see her again.

Chapter Twelve

TUESDAY BROUGHT A rush of customers, but with Parker and Robin working behind the counter, they handled the orders efficiently. It was the best start to a day that Raine could remember in months. That made her smile. Something she'd been doing all morning.

And not only because of her staff.

Raine sneaked a peek at Keaton, who worked on his laptop at the corner table. He'd arrived earlier than normal and let her pick another pumpkin spice drink for him.

She fought the urge to touch her forehead where Keaton had kissed her. For a practice date, last night had felt…real. She wasn't ready to open the door to dating yet. But leaving it ajar didn't feel wrong.

Not that Keaton wanted to push open the door and date her or vice versa. But she enjoyed spending time with him, and she hoped they could go out again.

As friends.

Or fellow Boo Bash volunteers.

Or…

A label wasn't necessary, even if she'd found herself labeling or being labeled quickly after she met someone. Raine didn't have to do things the way she'd always done them.

Going on the practice date last night had shown her that.

She glanced over at the corner table.

Keaton's screen blocked his keyboard, but she imagined his fingers typing at a rapid rate, the way she'd seen last week.

Click, click, click.

Words forming.

His eyes focused on the screen without a sense of anything around him.

She couldn't hear his fingers striking the keys, but in her head, the sound rose above the din of the other customers and the rhythm of his typing went with the beat of music playing.

Raine grinned. She hoped he was making good progress on his book.

Parker handed her a cup. "This is the last drink for the to-go order."

He was in his early thirties, from Portland, Oregon, where he'd managed a coffee franchise, and was willing to work any shift. He was quiet and hadn't given her a reason for moving to Silver Falls, but he showed up early, worked hard, and got along with everyone. She couldn't ask for anything more.

"Thanks." Raine put the café au lait into the drink carrier with three other cups. "Anna."

The dog groomer from Wags and Tails must be picking up coffee for the staff, only Callie's favorite drink was missing. She must be off or coming in later.

Someday I'll be able to do the same thing.

Maybe someday soon if her interviews this week went well.

As Anna came to the counter, her blond ponytail bounced. She tucked her phone into the front pocket of her hoodie. "Your smile's back."

"It's always been there."

"Not like this morning." Anna grinned. "Let me guess, it has something to do with Callie's brainy brother."

"He's helping me with the Boo Bash."

"I heard you went out last night. And he kissed you."

Seriously? "This town needs to watch TV or read more books."

Anna raised a curious brow. "So, it's true?"

"We went out for dessert."

Anna smirked. "Is he a good kisser?"

Raine glanced around to make sure no one was listening. "He kissed my forehead. No lips were involved."

"Too bad, but forehead kisses are so sweet. And a nice slow start to something more."

"It wasn't a date." Raine hated the way the words rushed out.

Anna shrugged. "Ask him out."

"He's only in town for a short time."

"Make the most of it," Anna encouraged.

"I…" Raine considered the idea and tossed it away. "I'm not ready to date again. And I've never done anything like that."

"Dated casually?"

She nodded.

Anna leaned in closer. "Look, I'm the last person to give relationship advice after what happened with Davis last Christmas."

"You're not clingy."

Raine couldn't believe Davis had called Anna that when they broke up. Of course, he changed his mind and wanted her back if they could date other people.

Who did that?

Well, besides Davis Tucker.

Raine respected Anna for saying no to the hottie contractor. Looks weren't everything.

Anna shrugged. "I wasn't trying to be, but he saw it that way. And I was desperate not to spend another holiday alone."

Raine would face that herself this year. Emmett and his family went all out with food and tradition. She'd enjoyed each holiday with them since moving to Silver Falls. From Thanksgiving through New Year, even Mrs. Wilson made her feel like one of the family, and for that, Raine was grateful. She would miss them.

"But I've changed my thinking about relationships after watching Callie and Brandt and Taryn and Garrett," Anna continued.

"Spill the tea please. Or is this secret sauce stuff?"

"A combination. We, I'm using that as a general term, need to stop trying to find a boyfriend."

"I'm not. I don't want one."

"Right now. But eventually you will." Anna sounded

more certain than Raine felt. "Relationships take on their own energy. You don't have to force anything. Love happens when it's right. I saw it with Callie and Taryn. That's what I'm holding out for."

"Even if it's a pipe dream?"

"It might feel like a pipe dream, but it's not. Some of us are just late bloomers."

"I prefer that to loser." Raine hadn't been called that, but she'd thought of herself as one after Emmett left her. Anna was all sunshine and smiles. "But you're younger than me."

"Life and love begin at thirty. That's my new motto and I'm sticking with it. I've told Pippa the same thing."

Anna would turn thirty-one soon. Raine smiled. "Going all in with this."

"One hundred percent. And I suggest letting things with the geeky gorgeous professor run their course, whether that's as friends, co-coordinators of the Boo Bash, or something more." Anna glanced over her shoulder toward the corner. "Should've called dibs in December."

"I didn't."

"He has eyes only for you. The same as Brandt had for Callie." Anna picked up the drink carrier. "Now relax, take a few deep breaths, and keep smiling."

"Thanks, Anna."

"You're welcome. I need to get these drinks to the shop while they're still warm, or Sam will complain."

Raine waved. "Have a great day. And thanks for the advice."

Now she had to put that into action.

Relaxing wasn't easy for Raine to do. Breathing deeply, she could handle. And smiling was something she did whenever she saw Keaton.

KEATON KEPT BUSY applying for jobs, working on the Boo Bash, and revising his manuscript. The Boo Bash took most of his time. He hadn't made it to the coffee shop yesterday, and earlier in the week, he'd arrived later in the day when the place was less crowded.

Not that Raine was less busy, but she appeared more relaxed and less tired now that Parker and Robin worked during the weekdays.

Progress.

Now to get the Boo Bash put together, so Raine would have less to worry about.

On Thursday at eleven, the first boxes of supplies he'd ordered arrived. Keaton carried the two boxes to the guest room and set them on the desk. He opened the first box—enough candy to send every dentist in Silver Falls on a fully paid, all excursions included Caribbean cruise. This amount was less than half the amount passed out during last year's Boo Bash. No wonder Robin and other parents wanted less candy given out. Next came the second box full of small toys and other items.

"It will be a bootiful Halloween in Silver Falls."

He double-checked his order with what arrived—candy, spider rings, jack-o'-lantern mini bubble bottles, sticky skulls, stretchy skeletons, mini coloring books, erasers, pencils, stamps, and stickers.

Keaton took a picture, typed a text, and hit *send*.

Me: Look what arrived.

Raine: Fun! That's a lot more than I thought we'd have.

Me: Wait until you see everything in person. Are you on break?

Raine: Yes. Can you bring the stuff to my house?

Me: When?

Raine: Tonight? I'm off at seven.

Me: See you then.

Keaton set the phone on the desk and put the items back into the boxes. He should bring something for her. The bakery was on the way, and most people enjoyed cookies. He would call ahead to see if someone knew what Raine enjoyed.

A knock sounded.

"Come in."

Rex lumbered into the room followed by Callie. "Margot let us in on her way out."

"Nice you could stop by." Rex pressed against Keaton. He'd seen the dog a few times since he arrived, but not as much as he'd planned. "Good to see my favorite nephew. Being good for your mom?"

Rex's tail wagged, and Keaton rubbed behind the dog's ear.

"He's always a good boy." Callie peered at all the supplies. "For the Boo Bash?"

Keaton nodded. "Just arrived."

"Looks like a lot of stuff. I didn't think the budget was that big."

It isn't. Keaton shrugged before brushing his hand through his hair.

"You bought some of this."

He picked up a bag. "Stretchy skeletons. How could I not?"

Callie's gaze clouded. She took a closer look at what was on the desk and in boxes. "You mentioned having savings—"

"I do. And severance." He raised his chin. "Don't worry, sis. This won't set me back."

"Okay, but why are you going to so much trouble? Spending your own money when you don't even live in Silver Falls and Margot forced you into helping?"

Raine had asked him a similar question. His answer remained the same, though there was more to it now. "The town is important to you and Garrett. That makes it important to me. Margot has opened her home to me for the second time this year. The First Avenue Business Association events mean everything to her. This is a perfect way to pay back her kindness and generosity."

"And Raine?"

Rex nudged Keaton's hand. The sign the dog wanted more rubs, so Keaton gave Rex what he wanted. "We agreed Raine needed help. A few have volunteered to do more than pass out candy at the Boo Bash, but it's only because they were asked. No one stepped up."

Callie's lips pursed. She blinked. "You're just helping Raine?"

That wasn't the question his sister wanted to ask. "I am, which is what Margot asked me to do. Everyone at the dinner thought it was a good idea."

Callie picked up a package of pencils. "Cute."

He focused on Rex, who savored each touch by leaning into Keaton more. The dog was addicted to rubs. "The Boo Bash will be fun."

"Looks like it." She set the pencils on the desk. "Are you having fun with Raine?"

"I haven't seen her much outside of the shop, but we'll work this weekend on the Boo Bash."

"You saw her Monday night at Lawson's."

That must be what was on Callie's mind. "We went for dessert."

A beat passed. Then another. "What was the forehead kiss all about?"

Talk about ridiculous. He sighed. "The people in this town really need to mind their own business."

"You're the one who kissed Raine on the sidewalk where everyone could see."

The words shot out of Keaton's mouth like Thor's Mjolnir. "Everyone?"

Callie shrugged.

"It was late. No one else was nearby or driving down the road. I'm not sure how anyone saw what happened."

"Security cameras."

His jaw dropped. "This town is whacked."

She plopped onto the bed. "It's a small town. But that's not the question here."

As soon as he stopped rubbing Rex, the dog nudged Keaton again. "It should be."

"Do you think kissing Raine was smart?"

"I'm not one to make dumb moves." He looked at Rex. "Isn't that correct? Uncle Keaton is smart."

Callie rolled her eyes. "Raine is…"

"Surprising. Funny. Sweet."

"Fragile."

He shook his head. "Not the Raine I know."

"Her and Emmett—"

"Raine's closed that door. She doesn't want to get back together with him."

Curiosity written all over Callie's face, she leaned forward. "How do you know?"

"She told me."

"Okay, but Emmett hurt Raine. Not once but multiple times. The guy led her to believe he would stay in Silver Falls, then tried to convince her to go with him. When she wouldn't, he dangled the long-distance-for-now carrot—twice."

"She didn't give me those details, but she was open about what happened."

"You're only in Silver Falls temporarily, so why are you dating her?"

"First, it wasn't a date. If it were, I would have kissed her on the lips not her forehead."

"If Raine thinks it's more—"

"Give me some credit, sis." Keaton couldn't believe this. "Raine knows I'm only in town for a short while. I've told her about losing my job."

Callie's eyes widened. "You told her?"

"I did, and she knows I'm applying for others."

"Oh." The one word spoke volumes.

"It's admirable you want to protect your friend. But Raine's an adult. Any other concerns we need to discuss?"

Callie did a double take. "Uh-oh."

Keaton shouldn't ask, but... "What?"

"You've got the look." She looked at Rex. "You see it too, right?"

Rex wagged his tail.

Something must be in the water source for Silver Falls. People acted weird. "What look?"

Callie studied him as if he were a new type of dog discovered and she was setting the breed standards. "It's the same one Garrett had when he talked or thought about Taryn."

Keaton made a T with his hands. "Time-out. I don't have any look. Again, what part of not a date did you miss, sis?"

"Just calling it like I see it, bro," Callie shot back.

"I hope you have health insurance with eye coverage. You need glasses."

She started to speak and then stopped herself.

Keaton knew that Callie was holding back. "Say what's on your mind, or you'll end up calling me in the middle of the night when you can't sleep."

"Okay, you're not wrong." Callie took a breath and another. "Please be careful with Raine. Even though you both know where things stand. She's been through a lot, and I worry about her. I'm not sure she can survive having her heart broken again."

Warmth balled in Keaton's chest. "You're a caring person, baby sis. I promise. I won't be breaking any hearts in Silver Falls, including Raine's."

Especially hers.

All he wanted to do was help her. Not hurt her.

He hoped Callie understood that.

A FEW HOURS later, Raine rinsed off her dinner plate and put it in the dishwasher next to two others. She usually only turned on the dishwasher once a week to not waste water. Often, she got takeout. One of the joys of being on her own was eating straight from the container.

She glanced around the house. Her clogs hadn't made it into the shoe basket again. The only things out of place were the three stacks of orange five-gallon plastic buckets, courtesy of Mr. Jones. He'd found them in his storage room and remembered he'd used them when he and Mrs. Jones ran the Boo Bash.

All she needed was…

Keaton.

Then they could get to work on sorting whatever had arrived and figure out the next steps.

The doorbell rang.

Her heart leapt. Okay, not really. It did a slight jump. Only because she wanted to see the things that had arrived.

Her bare feet padded across the floor. She opened the door.

Keaton stood next to two boxes. On top of them was another box she recognized from the local printer. He held out a bag from Lawson's Bakery. "I come bearing gifts."

"I see that." As Raine took the bag, the scent of chocolate and sugar tickled her nose. She could get used to being brought dessert. Even though she had a sweet tooth, it wasn't something she usually bought for herself. "Thanks. I had no idea you were bringing this much. I would have helped you carry it to the door."

He motioned to her feet. "No shoes. And it didn't take me long."

She set the cookie on a nearby end table. "The least I can do is help you bring the stuff in."

Keaton grabbed one of the larger boxes and the one from the printer. She got the other.

"See." Raine picked up the bag of cookies... Priorities! "I'll put these on a plate and get us drinks."

"I'll unpack." He glanced around. "Where do you want the stuff?"

"The dining room table so we can see everything."

"On it."

In the kitchen, Raine put the cookies on a plate. Not all were chocolate, but the scent of those made her mouth water. She blended whipping cream, pumpkin, pumpkin syrup, and pumpkin spice. Once that was mixed well, she used a hand mixer to make sure everything was nice and creamy. Ice went into two glasses. She added vanilla syrup to each and then cold brew coffee, which she'd made when she got home. Then she divided the pumpkin cream mixture between the two cups.

Raine wasn't a huge fan of pumpkin spice, but she enjoyed this drink. She carried them out of the kitchen.

Keaton's eyes widened. "Whoa. I heard the blender, but I had no idea you were going full-on barista tonight."

"Can't break your streak of trying new pumpkin spice drinks."

"That looks tasty."

She handed him one. "It's a Pumpkin Cream Cold Brew."

He took a sip. "Delicious."

"One of my favorite pumpkin spice drinks." And then she remembered. "Have a seat in the living room, and I'll get the cookies."

Raine hurried to the kitchen, grabbed the plate, and returned to the living room. Of course, she forgot napkins. But how messy could cookies be?

She placed the cookies on the table and sat, still holding her drink.

He raised his glass. "If you weren't already a barista, I'd say you missed your calling."

"Thanks. I used to make my parents' drinks on the weekends. I'd experiment with Dad's coffee and Mom's tea bags. I cut them open to make her special blends. I'm sure some mixtures were truly awful, but she drank every cup." Raine took a sip. The cream could be a tad thicker but not bad. "Got my first barista job, and there was no looking back."

"You found your passion early."

"I did." She set her cup on the table. "You did, too. A freshman in college is young."

He nodded. "The thing about teaching is we don't see the end results beyond the quarter or semester. Some students stay in touch if they think they'll need a recommendation letter someday but many you never see or hear from again."

"I get to see my finished project each time. And I can tell if someone likes it or not. Unless it's a to-go order. But in a small town, people come back if they enjoy something."

"That would be nice."

"Your book might be more immediate gratification, seeing people buy it and leave reviews."

"Unless the reviews are awful."

"I can't imagine you writing a bad book."

He leaned toward her. "Why is that?"

"You put everything into what you do. At least you have with the Boo Bash, so I assume you're writing would be the same."

"I hope you're correct."

Something told Raine she was. She took another bite of her cookie. "How is the book coming along?"

"Good, except…" He stared at his drink.

"What?"

"I have an outdoor scene. I'm struggling to come up with the right description. Which means I keep writing and rewriting. It's only a small part but an important one."

"Where have you been writing?"

"At Margot's and the coffee shop."

She thought for a moment. Keaton was intelligent. He probably knew this, but maybe he'd forgotten. "I journaled after I lost my parents as part of grief counseling. When the words wouldn't come, I would go to the park or lake. Being outdoors inspired me. You might need a change of scenery to find inspiration."

"That's a great idea."

"There are plenty of spots. The park is lovely this time of year with the leaves changing." She tried to think of other places when the perfect location hit her. "Have you been to Silver Falls?"

"No." He reached for a cookie. "I meant to when I was here in the summer, but the hike would have been too much for Rex, and I didn't want to leave him alone when he missed Callie so much."

The guy had a kind heart to care that much about a dog. "You should go. The hike has some gain in elevation, but you can make it to the falls in less than an hour. There are a few benches if you want to write there."

"Tomorrow, I want to pass out and hang flyers for the Boo Bash, but I could go on Saturday."

"It might be a little more crowded on the weekend, but if you can write at the coffee shop, that shouldn't bother you."

He nodded. "Would you want to go with me?"

The question caught her off guard. "To the falls?"

"Yes." He ate his cookie.

"I thought you wanted to write."

"I don't want to take my laptop on a hike. I can jot down some notes up there. You could bring a journal."

"I don't have one." The words flew out like the crows in the apple tree grove when the hawk kite had been installed. "My old one might be in a box in the attic. It's not something I've wanted to reread."

"Understandable." He rubbed his hands on his khakis. "You could still go. Maybe with the leaves changing colors, you'll get inspiration for a new autumn tea blend."

It sounded like he wanted company. "Well, it is my first full Saturday off. Timmy and Parker are working."

"Do you have other plans?"

"Only to not set an alarm and sleep in."

"I'm more of a planner, but I don't mind waiting until you're up. You need the sleep."

"I do." Saying anything else would be silly. "But a hike might be just the self-care I need."

"And the inspiration my creativity needs." His grin made him look more like a college student than a professor. "Text me when you wake up then we can figure out the time."

His eagerness to plan was adorable. "I will. And in the meantime, we need to go through all the stuff you bought and sort it. Mr. Jones gave us buckets, which will make it easier."

"That will make the job easy-peasy." Keaton pulled a piece of paper from his back pocket and unfolded it. "I made a list of which shop gets what."

"That will save us a ton of time. Thanks."

"Sometimes my being a planner comes in handy."

"It does." But did he plan out his life the same way? She might have to ask during their hike tomorrow. Right now, they had work to do.

Chapter Thirteen

THE DRIVE TO the trailhead on Saturday morning was quiet. Keaton focused on the road while Raine dealt with a problem at the coffee shop.

She lowered the phone. "Sorry about that."

"Need to go back?"

"Nope. Timmy has dealt with this before, but he's not on for another hour so Parker wasn't sure what to do."

"I had papers and exams to grade, office hours to keep, and emails to answer, but no one's ever called me at nine thirty on a Saturday with an emergency."

"The life of a business owner. If your company's bigger then there's more than one person to answer the phone. In my case, I'm it. But I don't mind. Well, not as much now that two new people have started, and I've hired two more."

"Congrats."

"Thanks. They're in high school so can't work during the day, but they'll take afternoon, evening, and weekend shifts. I have a few more interviews set up. More is less is my new motto."

He flipped on the blinker and turned left into the parking lot. "Must be a relief."

"Huge. October's only a week old, but it's a hundred times better than September."

Keaton hoped he was a part of the improvement this month. He parked at the trailhead. Three other cars were there. "We won't be on our own."

"This isn't bad." She unbuckled her seat belt and glanced over her shoulder at the other row of parking spots. "During the summer, you have to wait for a parking spot to open."

"We lucked out."

"The overcast skies help." She grabbed her backpack from her feet and slid out of his car. "Come on."

He got his pack from the back seat. "Didn't know we were in a hurry."

Raine had her backpack on. She wore cargo pants, a tech tee under a long-sleeved button-down shirt, and hiking boots. Nothing looked new, but she belonged out here. "What do you smell?"

Keaton inhaled. Nothing stuck out, though there was something a little sharp. Must be the trees surrounding them. "Pine?"

"Yes, but I smell rain."

"Smell rain?"

She nodded. "We should have time to make it to the falls and back if we don't dawdle."

Raine headed from the asphalt of the parking lot to the trailhead at a fast clip. Her hiking boots hit the dirt path.

He hurried to catch up to her. "That's a funny word for someone who slept in and wanted to take her time this morning."

She glanced over her shoulder with a cute smirk. "Hey, I wasn't dawdling. I was ready to go by nine thirty."

"So does one become a dawdler after ten?"

"Depends on the day and time and if—"

"You smell rain."

"You catch on fast."

Her grin lit up her entire face. Who needed the sun with Raine's smile? But for some reason she left him more off-balance today than usual.

"I'm trying." Around Raine, he wasn't sure he always succeeded. An odd feeling, but one he was getting used to. He considered himself smart, always had, but book smart wasn't the only kind of intelligence. Logically he'd known that, but he judged those without degrees or multiple degrees, including Callie. But street smarts and common sense counted, too. More so in some cases.

"Stop thinking so much and look around. We're outside. Nothing to do but soak in nature." Raine held out her arms and spun around. "Inspiration awaits, dear writer."

"You're not like this at the coffee shop."

"The whole business thing. And I've been so stressed with everything—that's made it harder to relax. But I've tried not to become a hard-nose boss."

He imagined Dean Fredricks, who'd run the college where his department had belonged with a metaphorical judge's gavel. "You're not. And you're right."

Trees flanked both sides of the trails. "It's beautiful out here."

She inhaled deeply. "It is. There are lots of places a short drive from Seattle when you want to get away, but Silver Falls is different. Special."

Keaton enjoyed seeing this side of Raine. No lines creased her forehead or formed around her mouth. He wished she could always be so carefree. "Gorgeous."

He didn't mean only their surroundings.

"Let inspiration take you wherever your muse needs to go. If you follow me, you'll get where you need to go."

Something in his chest shifted. Something he'd never felt before. "T-thanks," he croaked.

He followed her in silence. Birds chirped from the trees. Twigs snapped beneath their hiking boots. The higher they went, the sharper the scent of pine in the air became.

Keaton kicked a pebble. He imagined a troll getting hit and tempers flying. A fight would ensue. Nasty and for reasons that made no sense to anyone but trolls. That might work. "Do you mind if we stop for a minute?"

She did.

He pulled out a journal and pen. He wrote down ideas. Glimpses of what he saw around him and in his mind. He listed something from his other four senses. Satisfied, he tucked the items back into his pack's front pocket. "Thanks."

Raine beamed. "That's what we're here for. Ready to see the falls?"

"Lead the way." The falls would be the icing so to speak. A morning out there with Raine and scenery breathtaking enough to spark his creativity. It didn't get much better than that.

They continued up the path at a fast pace.

"When do you have time to work out?" he asked.

"I don't." She didn't slow. "Who needs a gym when I'm on my feet all day? I lift bags of coffee beans and other supplies. It keeps me in shape."

"I used to belong to a gym in L.A. That was my down time."

"There's nothing like that in Silver Falls, but Summit Ridge has a few places. The university, too."

Maybe he should have taken the barista job when she offered. If he had, he would be getting paid to work out. The best part was he would spend all day with Raine.

Rushing water sounded nearby. "We must be getting close."

"We are." The trail switched back. "It's just around the next bend."

His family had mentioned the falls once he'd brought them up, but he was happy to be there with Raine.

The water became louder. Keaton rounded the bend to see a huge waterfall cascading over rocks at the top and splashing up in a sea of mist and foam at the bottom. The gray rocks gave the water an almost silvery glow.

Mesmerized, he stared. "Silver Falls."

If the waterfall didn't inspire him, nothing would.

A family of four stood on the bridge closer to the water.

"It's not as impressive as Multnomah Falls in Oregon, but we're proud of Silver Falls."

"Someone was since they named a town after it."

"Yep." She pointed to a bench. "Sit and take it all in. See if inspiration hits."

It already had, but he wasn't sure if it was being out here or being with Raine. Maybe she was his muse.

And maybe he was getting caught up in the moment.

This was a hike, not a date or even a practice one.

"I will." He took a seat on the bench. A breeze carried mist toward him and wet his face. Not much, but just enough to make him feel alive. "What are you going to do?"

She had her phone out. "Take some photos."

Keaton focused on the falls, letting everything fall way. Soon he was writing page after page of notes. Some snippets of dialogue. Lines of description. The words flowed, and the scene giving him trouble made sense now.

Keaton wrote until he had nothing left to put on the page. He closed his journal.

He blinked, unsure where he was for a moment.

The falls came into focus. So did Raine, who stood on the bridge, her face lifted to the water cascading down.

He put away his pen and paper and made his way to her. "Get enough photos?"

She nodded. "You seemed in another place, so I came down here. Find inspiration?"

"Yes, thank you."

"Thank whoever discovered this place."

"That's you for me. I stand by my initial thank you."

His gaze held hers. Neither of them said anything. The roar of the falls provided the soundtrack. "I'm glad we came."

"Me, too, but unless you feel like getting soaked, we should head to the car."

Bummer. Keaton would have liked staying there longer. At least, she would be with him on the way back. "Lead the way."

If he wasn't having dinner with Brandt and Garrett tonight, Keaton would have asked Raine to go out with him.

Practice date or date didn't matter. Spending more time together did, Boo Bash or not.

THAT EVENING, RAINE sat at Callie's dining room table with her four closest friends in Silver Falls. In between them lay a casserole pan with what remained from their pasta dinner, their plates and utensils, a basket of bread, and an empty salad bowl.

Her muscles ached from the hike with Keaton, but they'd managed to just beat the rain, so the soreness was better than getting caught in the downpour. He'd needed to concentrate on the road during the drive home, which meant they didn't talk much. But she'd enjoyed every minute of the hike, especially watching the play of emotions cross his face as he wrote.

Magic.

That was the only way to describe what she'd seen today.

And that made her more excited for his book. She wasn't a huge reader, but she would make the time for his story.

Callie, Taryn, and Anna laughed at whatever joke Pippa told.

"Tired?" Taryn asked Raine.

"Just thinking." She raised her glass of Chardonnay. The

wine went well with the scallops in a white cream sauce served over pasta they'd eaten for dinner. "To Callie for a delicious meal and organizing a girls' night. It's been too long."

"Hear, hear!" Anna, Pippa, and Taryn cheered.

Callie blushed. "Thanks. It's about time we started doing these again."

This year, they hadn't had a chance to get together much. Callie and Anna had managed a few times with only the two of them, but their nights out—or in—had taken a back seat with all the changes in their lives.

"Well, now we need to keep it up." Anna sipped her wine. "I'm happy to host the next one."

"I'm in. Soon, I won't have to work weekends." Raine couldn't wait for that to happen. "I haven't been in all day today. Feels so good."

"Is Robin working out?" Callie asked, her voice quiet.

Nick Baxter had made life miserable for Brandt seven years ago and as recently as December. "She's a hardworking employee. Appreciative every hour she's scheduled. When Nick has the kids for the weekend, she asks to work weekends."

"I'm so happy for both of you." Callie grinned. "I still consider her a friend, even after what Nick did."

Taryn nodded. "Nick, Brandt, and I grew up together. Nick always wanted to be center of attention, but he was never mean about it. No one else cared. It was kind of joke. But he changed. The guy's a sociopath now."

"He's the one who named their dog, Precious. Reminds

me of Gollum in *Lord of the Rings*." Anna shuddered. "The dog looks so sweet, but she has a mean streak as long as Silver Falls."

No one knew Raine had spent the day with Keaton at the falls. She wanted to keep it quiet, if only to keep her friends from worrying about her.

Anna reached for an éclair. "I don't know either one of them well. But Robin's clothing and accessories make me green with envy."

"Go to the New Life consignment store in Summit Ridge." Raine debated between finishing her wine or eating one of Taryn's éclairs. "Robin dropped off a bunch of her stuff there."

Robin said Nick had lost their money investing in risky business ventures. He'd found a consulting job, but finances would be tight until their house sold. In the meantime, Robin hoped to sell enough items to cover renting an apartment for her and the kids.

Pippa wiped her mouth. "I know where I'm headed tomorrow. How about the rest of you?"

Callie beamed. "Brandt and I are having a picnic while we see the leaves change colors."

Anna had an of-course-you-are look. "I'm working in the morning. Mary Jo needs the time off. I'd love to go to the shop, but I'm staying away from Summit Ridge after bumping into Davis the other night."

"How was that?" Raine asked.

"Awkward." Anna reached for an éclair. "His date wore an engagement ring. Guess he decided to stop dating more than one person at a time."

Anna bit into the éclair.

"I'm so sorry," Pippa said.

Everyone else added their condolences, but no one was upset that Davis was no longer in Anna's life.

"She's welcome to him." Anna sighed. "It's just too bad there aren't many single men in the area. But I've got my patience cap on and deleted all my dating apps."

"I do have another brother." Callie got up to let Rex out.

"Grumpy, arrogant surgeon brother?" Anna made a face. "Hard pass, but thanks."

Taryn laughed. "Don't blame you for that. He's intense like my husband. I put him to work in the yard to get rid of some of that."

"What she's not saying is they're installing a dog run in the backyard," Callie confided.

"That too." Taryn gulped her wine.

"I've convinced them they need a dog." Callie winked. "They'd rather do that than have the wedding reception all the parents want to throw them."

"I married Garrett. That's all I wanted." Taryn sounded adamant. "I don't need a reception."

"A wedding cake would be nice," Anna said. "I could put a slice under my pillow and dream about my future spouse."

"I'll make you a wedding cake," Taryn replied. "No reception required. Everyone can take home a slice to eat or sleep on."

"If there's no wedding, does it count as a wedding cake?" Callie asked.

Taryn shook her head.

"How are things going with the professor?" Anna asked Raine.

"We've been working on the Boo Bash." Keaton had handed out most of the flyers. "He has great ideas."

Pippa smiled. "I don't think Anna was asking about the Boo Bash."

"I wasn't," Anna chimed in.

"We went hiking to Silver Falls earlier today, but that wasn't a date or anything. We're just working on the Boo Bash and hanging out."

"Isn't that how you ended up with Emmett, only not with the Boo Bash as the catalyst?" Taryn asked.

Yes, but… Raine shrugged. "Keaton isn't like Emmett."

"He's better-looking," Anna muttered.

She wasn't wrong. "Keaton's not sticking around Silver Falls. But doing things with him is good practice for when I'm ready to date again."

"Emmett's dating already," Pippa said.

"I know, but I'm not him," Raine clarified. "I mean, I'm over Emmett. But I'm not ready."

Callie refilled her wineglass. "I owe Keaton an apology."

"What for?" Anna asked.

Raine wanted to know the answer to the question.

"I was worried he might hurt you," Callie said to Raine. "But he said the same thing you just said."

"Thanks, but I'm not letting Keaton or anyone else in."

Taryn grabbed an éclair. "Sometimes what you want isn't what you need."

"It is in my case." Raine appreciated her friends, but they were wrong in this case. Yes, she was attracted to Keaton. They had fun together. There seemed to be a spark between them. That didn't happen every day, but the timing was off. "And besides, we're too different."

True, but saying the words left a hollow feeling inside her. She didn't want more, but there seemed to be a connection with Keaton.

"What do you mean different?" Taryn asked.

Oh, boy. Raine hadn't wanted to go there.

Her four friends stared at her as if they were looking at a complete stranger.

Guess I'm going there. Raine took a breath. "We're opposites. Keaton's a professor. He has three college degrees. The definition of smart. I'm a barista who barely passed to get her associate's degree."

"A degree doesn't make someone smart. You own and run your own business. You couldn't do that if you weren't intelligent."

"I attended a culinary institute to learn to be a pastry chef. That was better for what I wanted to do than getting a college degree."

"Seriously better," Pippa agreed. "I have a degree in horticulture. It's come in handy, but I spent a lot of money when I could have learned the information elsewhere. I would have been better off getting a degree in business. I'm still paying off my student loans."

"Pippa's right." Callie scooted forward in her chair. "I have a degree I'm doing nothing with. I didn't have to pay for college, but it was a waste of my parents' money given what I do now. Don't sell yourself short."

"Do you really feel this way?" Anna asked. "Or is it how Emmett made you feel after things ended?"

Raine considered the questions. "A little of both. Silver Falls was no longer good enough for him. And when he called it quits with me the last time, I wasn't good enough for him either."

"Not true," Callie blurted.

"Feels true," Raine admitted.

"Emmett wanted a different future." Taryn smiled sympathetically at Raine. "That's not on you."

"It's hard to believe that." Raine stared into her wineglass. "I believed in forever with Emmett, but my dreams turned into nothing. Maybe I'm not supposed to have a forever with someone."

"Or maybe you just haven't met the right person," Taryn said with compassion.

Callie nodded. "Someone is out there for you, Raine. The same as for Anna and Pippa."

Someone. Not Keaton.

Was Raine reading too much into this? Those éclairs looked mighty tasty. Forget the wine. She wanted sugar.

Anna tsked. "You're sounding like Margot, Callie."

Callie raised her shoulders. "Well, she brought me and Brandt together."

"And me and Garrett," Taryn added.

"Coincidence," Pippa spoke in a firm tone.

Callie shrugged. "Maybe, but that's two of five of us."

"Nope." Anna shook her head. "Not buying it."

"Please don't fuel Margot's matchmaking," Raine said. "If Margot thinks something is happening between Keaton and I, she'll be beaming brighter than the lights on Broadway, and trying her matchmaking skills on others. This conversation can't leave this room."

The others agreed.

"Now," Raine said. "Can someone please pass me an éclair?"

Death from Lawson's Bakery sounded like a good idea. The only problem? She wanted to share with Keaton.

IN THE ONLY bar in Silver Falls, Keaton lined up the cue and hit the white ball. It struck the three-ball, which rolled and dropped into the corner pocket. "That's how it's done, gentlemen. Three more, and I win."

Garrett rolled his eyes. "Lucky shot, little brother."

Brandt groaned. "No one told me I'd be hustled tonight."

"Hey, no one's hustling." They were playing six-ball. The object—put the balls into the pocket in order from one to six. Keaton hadn't shot off the break, which had made taking over and gaining control easier. "I can't help it if I'm a pro at pool."

Even though Keaton had been up half the night writing, he wasn't tired. If anything, the words exhilarated him.

He took another shot. The four-ball went in easy.

"Hustler," Brandt muttered.

Garrett laughed. "Guess this is what they teach in college these days."

"You'd be surprised." Keaton studied the angles for the best shot to knock the five-ball in. Math was his least favorite subject—chemistry held second place, but geometry came in handy playing pool. He tapped the white ball with his cue. That sent the orange ball banking off the far side and into the middle hole. "One more to go."

Brandt shook his head. "Your little brother doesn't play fair."

Keaton figured out his shot for the six-ball. He took aim and…

Garrett snickered. "Wonder what Raine thinks of gambling."

The cue didn't hit where Keaton intended. Who was he kidding? The white ball missed the green ball completely. It wasn't even close. "You distracted me."

Brandt grinned like the only turkey left at the farm before Thanksgiving. "I'd say a certain barista's name did that."

"Heckling isn't against the rules because there are no rules." Garrett took aim. With one tap of his cue to the white ball, he sunk the six. "Now, that's how it's done."

"I need another beer." Keaton headed to the bar.

The other two followed him.

He ordered another round.

"So you and Raine?" Brandt asked.

"He's helping her with the Boo Bash," Garrett said.

Brandt laughed. "Guess I know more than big brother for once."

The bartender placed three pints of lager on the bar. Brandt handed them out.

"Wait." Garrett held his glass. "You and Raine are going out?"

Keaton took a sip. The cold liquid went down smoothly. "No. We're not dating, but we've been hanging out. Someone saw me kiss her forehead in a security tape, and the rumors have been flying ever since."

Garrett's brows drew together. "Raine knows you're leaving, right?"

"It's never been clearer that Callie truly is your mini-me. That should scare me more than it does." Brandt drank.

Garrett's jaw jutted forward. "What's that supposed to mean?"

"Callie's worried Keaton is leading Raine on," Brandt answered before Keaton could.

"Are you?" Garrett asked a beat later.

"No." Keaton didn't know why everyone was so worried about Raine. The woman was so much stronger than people gave her credit for. "Raine knows what happened with my job and that I'm applying for a new one. I've been upfront about leaving Silver Falls. Satisfied?"

Garrett nodded, but his entire posture was tight like it was jury selection day. "Just be careful. You won't be around here long, but the rest of us will have to live with the consequences of your actions."

Keaton rolled his eyes. "No consequences, bro. I'm sure you've heard of swipe left and right. Those of us in ivory towers even participate in such activities as hanging out or spending time with someone you get along with."

"True." Garrett took a swig of beer. "But Raine doesn't strike me as the casual dating type."

"She admitted she's not, but that's not what we're doing so it's a nonissue." Keaton didn't want to tell them about her not knowing how to date and the practice one that set off all the gossip. "Trust me. She's on board with this. One hundred percent."

Brandt shook his head. "He sounds like Callie except for the deeper growly voice."

That brought a laugh. Still, Keaton pinned his brother with a hard stare. "You might live in Silver Falls now, but I spent six weeks here this summer. That's five weeks longer than you were here for the wedding. Give Raine some credit. She's a grown woman, who is fine with what's happening. If she wasn't, she would stop it."

"That's true," Brandt agreed. "Raine can take care of herself, which is what I told Callie."

"Thanks for having my back." Keaton raised his glass to his brother-in-law. "You're right."

"Hope you're both correct." Garrett, however, didn't sound convinced. "It's clear you're not serious about her."

Keaton flinched. "How do you know that?"

"If you cared about Raine, you wouldn't be so flippant in the way you talk about her. You would have shut down this conversation as soon as it began."

Brandt stared over his beer glass. "True that."

Both were wrong. Keaton did care about her, or he wouldn't have spent all day Friday going to every business in

Silver Falls, including the market, asking them to put up the flyer.

He took a drink.

Flippant?

Keaton hadn't been flippant. People had it all wrong, acting like Raine was a fragile porcelain doll when she was strong and independent. Those characteristics were finding their way into his story's female protagonist.

Raine was both, or she never would have survived losing her parents, moving to a new town, and starting a coffee shop. But he wasn't about to say that to Garrett and Brandt. That wasn't being uncaring or flippant. The reason was the simplest of all—it was no one's business.

Chapter Fourteen

KEATON SAT AT Raine's dining table, filling a bucket with bat stamps, candy, and instructions. The type of activity he'd been doing most nights for a week and a half. She'd even given him a key to her house so he wouldn't have to wait when she got held up at the coffee shop. This was the first key to a woman's place he'd ever had. Keaton appreciated her trust.

He glanced at Raine, who sat across from him, separating the Halloween stamps and placing them in plastic baggies. He placed one set of those—bat stamps for the hardware store—on top of the candy filling the orange bucket.

"I hope this is simple enough for Mr. Jones." Simple for this year's Boo Bash equaled passing out candy and stamping kids' scavenger hunt list with a specific item or character. "He specified something uncomplicated on his form."

"He'll be fine." Raine stretched her arms over her head. "Mrs. Jones was at the coffee shop yesterday. She'll be at the hardware store to help during the Boo Bash."

"I'm glad we cut the pumpkin decorating there."

"That would have been the opposite of simple."

Keaton nodded. Only one week to go until B-Day, what

he'd been calling the date of the Boo Bash, and over half the buckets were ready to be delivered to shops. If they kept up the same pace, they'd be finished this weekend, which meant no last-minute work or late nights to be ready on time.

"I plan to be at the coffee shop tomorrow." Some of the prep work involved things he couldn't do there. "I have a couple of things to do in the morning, but the afternoon is reserved for book writing."

"Still inspired?"

He nodded. "I keep forcing myself to go to bed. I'd be happy writing through the night, but I'd regret it the next day when I'm tired."

"Now you know where to go again if you're having trouble."

"I do." Only he wasn't certain whether being outdoors at the falls had been the deciding factor or being there with Raine. Keaton guessed he would figure that out eventually.

They hadn't spent as much time together in the same place, but they'd texted daily, often several times a day.

Her cell phone rang. The ringtone was from a song. Something by Taylor Swift. Callie used to listen to it a lot, but he didn't remember the song's name.

Raine glanced at her phone, sitting face up on the table. She inhaled sharply.

None of his business, but he looked.

Emmett's name appeared on the screen.

First a text. Now, a phone call.

Had Emmett tried to reach her again when Keaton wasn't there? Were things escalating between the former couple? Or had Raine had a change of heart over her ex?

Keaton's gut churned. A yes to any of those questions wouldn't be good.

For Raine.

Not good for Raine.

She hit the decline button on the screen.

Keaton leaned back in his chair. That was interesting.

"Sorry." She rubbed her thumbs over her fingers. "I didn't want to put my phone on silent mode in case someone at the shop needed me. Nick has the kids, so Robin wanted to close."

"Phones ring." Keaton wanted to wipe away the worry from her eyes. "I saw who was calling."

She glanced at the now-dark screen. "Yes."

"You didn't answer."

"No." The word came out clipped. "I have nothing more to say to him."

Keaton shouldn't, but he had to ask. "Don't you want to...lock the door?"

Her lips parted. "Shouldn't no answer be an answer by default?"

"Not sure if everyone sees it that way."

"I would."

Knowing she didn't want to talk to her ex made Keaton happy. Raine deserved better. "Has he been trying to contact you and open the door?"

"Not since the text."

"Good, I mean—"

"It is good," she finished for Keaton. "Emmett's the one

who left for the Emerald City."

"Oz?"

"No, Seattle. But for me, there's no place like home."

"Silver Falls."

She nodded. "Emmett lived in Silver Falls his entire life. He planned on leaving, but then I moved to town to open the coffee shop, and he stayed. I thought we were on our way to a happily ever after, but he wasn't happy. He wanted to leave Silver Falls and asked me to go with him, but…"

"You couldn't."

"Not only couldn't. I didn't want to. Not even for my happy ending."

"Was that hard for you?"

"Yes and no. The fact I didn't consider going makes me realize we weren't meant to be. But I'd grown up in a suburb of Seattle, lived there until I moved here, but it never felt like Silver Falls. Long distance didn't work. When Emmett decided he was finished with Silver Falls and me in April, I won't claim it didn't hurt. That it didn't take me a while to get out of my funk, but the last time I saw him in July, I knew for sure. We're better apart. He's happier in Seattle. And when I'm ready for another relationship, it'll be with someone who wants the same things as me."

Keaton considered her words. "You found your home and don't want to leave. I'm still searching for mine."

"You'll find it." She covered his hand with hers. "You're where you should be. Silver Falls is the perfect place to search for a new home."

"I'm open to suggestions."

"I have one, but first, you should know it's not as hard as it sounds if you keep an open mind."

"That doesn't sound hard."

"It's not if you trust yourself."

"What do you mean?" he asked.

"As you search, you'll come across a lot of different places. But when you find the one…home…there will be a sense of belonging inside of you. You won't feel the need to look for something better. Everything you could ever want is right there. Mind you, it might not be perfect, but that doesn't matter. You'll be content and at peace, even when things don't go the way you wanted."

Keaton had a feeling she meant Emmett. "So, when you know you know?"

"Yep." Her mouth quirked. "As for actual suggestions, with your family here, Silver Falls or Summit Ridge should be on your list of places to consider. And no Washington state income tax is a huge plus. There's also a community college and a four-year university nearby. The cost of living is lower than you'll find in Seattle, the Vancouver-Portland Metro area, or Spokane."

He laughed. "You sound like a town spokesperson or Margot."

Raine looked at her hand on his. Her lips parted as if she hadn't realized she was touching him, and she lifted her hand from his. "Has Margot been trying to get you to stay in Silver Falls?"

Keaton missed Raine's touch. "Yes. Garrett and especially Callie have been, too, though they're more subtle."

"Margot's not known for her subtlety."

"She means well."

"Can't disagree with that since Margot brought you to help with the Boo Bash."

"There's no place I'd rather be than working on it with you."

All he wanted to do was kiss her. But they both had places to be and a stack of things to review was still on the table. "So you ready to keep going?"

She nodded. "We have time for a few more buckets tonight."

That gave him an idea. "What do you say when we finish we celebrate by going out to dinner?"

"Another practice date?" she teased.

"We can call it whatever you want, even a real date, if you're ready to move on."

She bit her lip.

Keaton hoped he hadn't pushed her too much. "Or we can stick to practicing."

Raine stared up through her eyelashes in a way that made her both vulnerable and sexy at the same time. "For real might be nice."

His pulse kicked up. Very nice. But he didn't say that. "We can decide later."

She nodded. "Guess that gives us incentive to finish a few more buckets tonight."

"It does."

Awareness buzzed between them. Unexpected but not unwelcome. This could get interesting.

STIFLING A YAWN, Raine stood at the shop's cash register. She'd had two Saturdays off and was used to sleeping late. This morning's alarm had been a shocker. She rang up Mr. Hurley's order. "That'll be six-eighteen."

He paid using a card.

The approval came through. "Your order will be ready soon."

This morning wasn't that busy, but that might change in an hour.

"Thanks." Mr. Hurley, who operated the Christmas tree lot in December, ran a small stand on the weekends selling the fruit and nuts from his other trees. "I'm hearing good things about the Boo Bash."

"Should be fun." Raine couldn't believe it was only five days away. Time was flying by, but she had enjoyed every minute working with Keaton. She should be doing that with him today and finishing the final buckets.

Except she had to be here.

Robin had called late last night saying Nick dropped off the kids, who both had a stomach bug, so she could take care of them. Clean up the mess was what he'd really meant. But Raine understood custody issues and how things might not go smoothly each time. She'd told Robin not to worry, to keep washing her hands so she didn't get sick, and that her shift would be covered.

Raine restocked the display unit with more scones and muffins.

"I can handle this place on my own." Timmy prepared a

caramel macchiato. "There's no reason for you to be here."

"You run this place better than I do." Though Parker was catching on fast. "But I prefer to have two people."

"It's your day off."

"And if Parker can come in later, I'll leave." He was busy this morning. "If not, you're stuck with me."

"I don't mind that. It's just…"

"What?"

"Just a sec." He placed the drink on the counter. "Mayor Sellwood."

The mayor in a track suit and ponytail came to the counter. She picked up her drink. "Looking forward to the Boo Bash, Raine."

"Should be fun." That had become Raine's stock answer. Saying it would be awesome might raise expectations, so people ended up disappointed. Fun seemed the best adjective to use.

"Mr. Hurley," Timmy called out.

The tree farmer grabbed his drink. "See you at the Boo Bash."

Raine waved.

The lull in customers gave her a chance to drink her own coffee.

"So back to what I was saying." Timmy took a swig from a water bottle. "Ever since Heather left and Robin and Parker started, you look better. Happier. More rested. I don't want you to go back to being overworked and exhausted."

"One Saturday won't change anything. I promise."

His nose scrunched. "Aren't you supposed to work with

Keaton today?"

"Yes, but we can do it tomorrow." She'd texted him last night to give him a heads-up that she wouldn't be home. "Sometimes people need to call out. This is nothing like Heather."

Timmy shivered. "We should call her she-who-can't-be-named."

"She was that bad, wasn't she?"

He nodded. "The worst."

They both laughed.

Timmy winked. "Be glad you have me."

He was too much, but what he said was true. "I count my blessings each and every day."

The bell on the door jingled.

"And our impromptu break's over," Timmy whispered.

She smiled, only her smile got bigger when she saw Keaton and Garrett. "Hey."

"Good morning." The way Keaton gazed into her eyes, making her feel like the only person in his world, told her it would be a great day. "I wanted to see if it was okay if Garrett came with me to your house to finish the buckets today."

"You're working on them."

"Yes," Garrett answered for Keaton. He motioned to his brother. "This guy woke me up early but said we had to stop here first for your permission."

Keaton rolled his eyes. "You don't invite someone into another person's house without permission."

"As if I'll steal something or make a mess."

"Asking is the right thing to do." Keaton focused on Raine again. "Do you mind?"

Her heart melted. "I don't. Help yourself to what's in the kitchen."

Garrett raised a box. "My wife is providing breakfast."

"I can provide coffee," Raine offered. "What would you like?"

"One of those pumpkin spice drinks Keaton can't stop raving about," Garrett said.

Raine stood taller. That was the best compliment she could have received. She looked at Keaton. "Do you want one you've already had?"

"What's next on the list?"

"A Nitro Cold Brew with Pumpkin Cream Cold Foam."

"Love the other pumpkin cream, but it's a little chilly out for that. How about the Pumpkin Spice Flat White?"

Garrett snickered. "Listen to my little brother order fancy coffees."

"Ignore him," Keaton said. "My second oldest brother can't be nice until his first cup of coffee."

Garrett nodded. "He's not wrong."

"Two Pumpkin Spice Flat Whites coming up."

Garrett had his wallet out. "How much?"

Raine held up her hands. "No charge. Boo Bash volunteers get drinks on the house."

"If I'd known that, I would have offered to help sooner."

Keaton scoffed. "You didn't offer today. Your lovely wife suggested you help me. You came kicking and screaming."

Andrews family get-togethers must be interesting.

"Timmy will have your order up shortly."

Garrett moved to the far end of the counter and spoke to Timmy, who made their drinks.

"Thanks." Keaton leaned over the counter. He kept his voice low. "As soon as we finish, I'm making a dinner reservation for us. How does the Falls Café sound?"

"Great." She fought the urge to shimmy her shoulders. "It's my favorite place in town."

"I can't wait to celebrate all the buckets being done."

Her pulse quickened as if she'd downed two espresso shots. She couldn't wait to go out with Keaton again. "Me, too."

Their gazes met.

"Drinks are ready, Keaton," Timmy called out.

"I'll text you."

"Have fun."

Keaton and Garrett walked out with their drinks. Keaton waved at her, and she waved back.

Timmy crossed his arms over his chest. A swatch of purple hair fell over his left eye. "Guess there's another reason you're happier, besides hiring Robin and Parker."

"Huh?"

"You and the professor." Timmy's suggestive tone left no room for misinterpretation. "You've always had a crush on him."

"I'm too old for a crush. And he's not my type."

"I agree. He's not. Keaton's the opposite of Emmett and perfect for you."

"He's..." She struggled to find the right words. "He's

not staying in Silver Falls. He's helping me with the Boo Bash."

"That look you two shared?" Timmy touched his chest. "A thousand heart-eye emojis rose to the ceiling. More than the Boo Bash is happening."

"We've hung out."

Timmy's eyes narrowed. "Define hang out."

"Dessert at Lawson's and hiking to Silver Falls."

"He mentioned dinner."

"Hasn't happened yet."

"But it will. Are you sure this is a good idea? You said you would never do long distance again."

"Don't worry. It's not like that with Keaton. He's been upfront about looking for jobs and leaving Silver Falls. But this is good practice for when I'm ready to date again."

"Practice, okay." Timmy didn't sound like he believed her. "Just be careful. I remember when you met Emmett, and you two came together fast. But I never saw you look at him the way you look at Keaton."

"Gratitude," she blurted. She was grateful for his help. That was all it could be, right?

Chapter Fifteen

O N SUNDAY NIGHT, Keaton knocked on Raine's front door. Pippa's flower shop was closed, so he'd grabbed a bouquet of mixed flowers from the market. The vibrant flowers reminded him of Raine. She wore black or blue jeans and dark T-shirts to work, but her house was light and bright.

The door opened.

Raine wore a brown lace dress, topped with a black shawl, and brown ankle boots. He liked the look. This was the first time he'd seen her not in leggings or pants. Several long necklaces, all different, draped around her neck. Long dangling earrings graced her earlobes and the size of the other earrings got smaller as they went up her ears. Her hair was fluffier, almost curly. But her easy smile and warm eyes were his favorites.

"You're stunning." He remembered the bouquet and handed it to her. "These are for you."

Her lips parted, and then a wide grin spread across her face. She sniffed the flowers. "They're beautiful. Do I have time to put them in water?"

He nodded. "I'm early."

"I planned for that."

Huh? What did she mean by that?

"Come in." She headed toward the kitchen where she removed a vase from the cabinet above the stove. She filled the vase with water, added the plant food that had come with the bouquet, clipped each stem using scissors, and placed the flowers in the vase. "They're beautiful. Thank you."

She was the beautiful one. "Is your dress vintage?"

"Sort of. It's made from vintage pieces. I found an online store who makes dresses like these and fell in love. I don't dress up much, but when I do I wear stuff like this."

It sure beat a boring sweater set and skirt. Was it getting warm in here?

"Ready to go?" she asked.

He nodded. Maybe he'd feel more like himself when they arrived at the café.

Raine locked the door and then they headed toward his car. As he walked behind her, his gaze zeroed in on a vine tattoo that rose from her boot, wrapped around her calf, and snaked up beneath the hem of her dress. Initially he'd noticed her tattoos, but over the past month, he no longer saw them. They'd just been a part of her. But now that he saw this new one, he wondered how high it went or if there was a meaning behind it. That surprised him. He wasn't into tattoos himself, but Raine's intrigued him.

Okay, distracted him. And he had to admit her tattoos and jewelry appealed to him more than pearls.

THE FALLS CAFÉ was Raine's favorite place to eat in Silver Falls. A bud vase with a single red rose and a flickering votive sat on the linen-covered tablecloth. The food had been mouthwateringly delicious, as usual. The service impeccable. But she'd never had a more enjoyable time than tonight.

The difference?

Keaton.

They'd talked nonstop since they left her house. The only breaks in conversation had been when they ate, but the silence was comfortable rather than awkward. Now that the plates had been removed, they continued talking.

He took a sip of water. "So a few freshmen, especially the gamers, were floored that Thor and Loki weren't OG in comic books. They went into complete denial, which wasted an entire class when I'd hoped to cover all the Norse gods because they wanted to show me the movies the characters were in."

She laughed. "I thought your students were the best and the brightest."

"Some must slip through the cracks."

"Or maybe they live sheltered lives."

"Possibly. Enough about my classroom tales." Keaton reached across the table and laced his fingers with hers. "Tonight is a celebration. We did it. All the prep for the Boo Bash is completed."

Raine stared at their linked hands. She should be more weirded out, but his touching her felt totally natural. "We work well together."

"We do."

"Raine?" a woman asked.

Emmett's mom stood near their table with a shocked expression on her face. "Hi, Mrs. Wilson."

Mrs. Wilson's brows knotted. "Um, hello. Who's your friend?"

"Keaton Andrews, this is Mrs. Wilson. Mrs. Wilson, this is one of Callie's brothers."

Keaton flashed her a polite yet practiced smile. "Nice to meet you, Mrs. Wilson."

Mrs. Wilson's mouth formed a perfect o, but her gaze remained locked on Keaton's hand on Raine's. "Emmett told me he's been trying to reach you."

Raine schooled her features, not wanting to show her surprise. Mrs. Wilson had never been antagonistic, but gossip had gotten back to Raine that Emmett's mom thought he could do better. Though Mrs. Wilson had been upset when her son left town. "I've been busy at the shop and planning the Boo Bash."

Keaton raised her hand and kissed the top of it. "And spending time with me."

Mrs. Wilson's eyes nearly bugged out.

"I have." Raine owed Keaton for helping with the Boo Bash, but his actions tonight earned him dessert. She would be buying at Lawson's the next time. "I heard Emmett's seeing someone. I hope that's going well for him."

"Of course, it is." Mrs. Wilson stared down her nose. "My Emmett is a catch."

Raine kept a smile frozen in place. Mrs. Wilson had told her after the breakup there were plenty of fish in the sea.

"So is Raine," Keaton said, not letting go of her hand.

She would order him an extra scoop of ice cream if he wanted pie—or whipped cream if he got something else. Whatever he wanted.

Mrs. Wilson continued to stare. It was uncomfortable and weird.

"We were just leaving," Raine said. "See you."

Emmett's mom walked away.

"Is she gone?" Raine asked.

"Peeking around the corner," Keaton whispered back. "Was that as weird for you as it was for me?"

"Weirder. I've spent every holiday for the past four years at her house. She was happy when Emmett broke up with me, but she acted surprised that I was with you."

"Not surprised. Upset."

"You think?"

He nodded. "I'm surprised steam wasn't coming out of her ears."

"Don't know why." Raine forced herself not to look at anything but him. "Emmett's living his best life. Why shouldn't I?"

"Am I part of your best life?"

"Yes, I mean…"

"I'm happy to be part of it for now, okay? And sorry if I overdid the date stuff."

"You were the perfect date. Want to head over to Lawson's? My treat."

Keaton squeezed her hand. "That's an offer I can't refuse."

"Let's go."

Outside as they headed toward the bakery, they held hands.

"You're quiet," he said.

"Dinner was great. Even with the unexpected visitor. I'm going to be sad when the Boo Bash is over."

"I'd like to keep seeing you while I'm in town."

Her spirits soared. "Any idea how long that will be?"

"No, is that okay?"

"To hang out and have fun?"

He nodded.

She was more of a relationship type, but temporary with an end date not that far away would be good for her. Practice for when she was ready for a boyfriend again. "Does that mean you expect free coffee?"

"Oh, I plan to keep coming in for more of your special pumpkin spice drinks. That's a given. But free isn't."

"We can discuss that. But I'm up for taking things day by day until you leave."

"Thank you." He stopped. "Can we seal our deal with a kiss?"

The hope in his voice melted a piece of her heart, but she wanted to be sure what he was asking. "A practice one?"

"For real."

Raine nodded.

He lowered his head to hers. She met him halfway. Their mouths met and…

His lips were soft and warm and oh-so-sweet. From his after-dinner drink, yes, but there was something more. Extra.

Him.

Keaton kept holding on to her hand, but his free arm wrapped around Raine. He pressed harder against her lips. Tingles exploded at the point of contact and shot outward in all directions.

Wowsa.

Forget bad boys. The professor's kissing expertise beat them all. Raine wanted to keep on kissing him.

A warning bell sounded in her head.

She took a step back. Her heart galloped like it had finished running the Kentucky Derby.

Wide-eyed, Keaton's ragged breathing matched her own. He appeared at a loss for words.

That made two of them.

But they couldn't stand there all night staring at each other.

"We should get to Lawson's." Though she doubted any dessert could beat his toe-curling kiss. Not that Raine remembered curling her toes, but she probably had given the tingles.

A peace settled over her. She'd closed the door to relationships and love thanks to Emmett, but Keaton was pushing that door open. If only…

No, she had to take things day by day. Even if her heart, and now her lips, wanted…more.

THE DAY BEFORE the Boo Bash, Keaton sat at his usual table with an iced vanilla chai with pumpkin cream cold foam drink. He raised his glass in a salute to his revised manuscript. He'd gone over the entire thing yesterday to make sure it was ready. His heart told him it was.

Time to send his story out into the world.

He attached it to the email reply from the agent he'd queried. She'd requested the full manuscript.

"Nothing to lose, and everything to gain." Keaton glanced at Raine behind the counter, and his chest expanded. He pressed *send*. "And it's off."

"Yo, Keaton." Brecken strode over in a hoodie with a baseball cap turned backward. He shrugged off his backpack and sat. "I got a B-minus on my paper. Highest grade so far."

He gave Brecken a high five. "Congrats."

"Couldn't have done it without you. Like seriously because I would have just watched the movie."

"Didn't you get more out of the book?" Keaton asked.

"A lot more. Except reading took me a lot longer."

"There are audiobooks. Check the library if the college doesn't have them," Keaton suggested. "Listening is easier for you."

"I will."

Timmy, today with hot pink hair, came over to the table with two drinks. He placed them on the table and sat.

"Tell him," Brecken urged Timmy.

"I got an A-minus on my assignment. The professor said he was impressed with my organized thoughts." Timmy settled in his chair. "He wants to keep a copy for his records."

"That's wonderful." Keaton was proud of both young

men. He raised his drink. "To writing papers and getting good grades."

The three cheered and drank.

Raine cleaned off a nearby table. She shot a smile Keaton's way.

Brecken sighed. "I wish you were my instructor, Keaton."

"Same." Timmy fiddled with the cup sleeve. "I'd love to have you as my professor at Summit Ridge. You're better than any of the ones I have."

Keaton appreciated their gratitude, but... "Thanks, guys."

"Transfer to Summit Ridge." Brecken leaned over the table. "Students transfer to other colleges, so I'm guessing professors can too."

Timmy nodded. "Yeah, and you'd be closer to your family in Silver Falls."

Brecken tilted his head. "Your parents and Flynn are in L.A., but they don't seem to mind visiting Silver Falls."

Timmy kept nodding as if that would convince Keaton. "Everyone would take your classes."

"Scandinavian Folklore and Legends might not be that cool to the students at Summit Ridge."

"You make them cool."

"Thanks." The compliments meant a lot to Keaton.

Raine had wiped the same table a few times.

"Pull out your homework," he said. "You don't want to be here studying all night."

"Keaton must have a big date tonight," Brecken teased.

Keaton did, but that was none of their business. Especially since it was with Margot.

"Hit the books," Keaton said. "Rule number one of study club, don't question the professor."

Brecken snickered. "That means he's got a date."

"A hot date." Timmy glanced at Raine, who returned to the counter.

Keaton downed the remainder of his drink. "I'm getting a refill."

Timmy stood. "I'll get it."

"This is your study time." Keaton stood. "Be right back."

At the counter, he handed over his cup. "Can I have another?"

"Sure." Raine prepared the new one. "Why didn't you tell the kids the truth about why you won't teach at Summit Ridge?"

"What truth?"

"It's a state school."

She was correct, but… "I would never say that to them. Summit Ridge is the perfect college for Timmy. It'll be a good fit for Brecken."

"But not you?"

"I've always had a dream…"

"Tier one. I know."

"It's what I want. Is that wrong?"

"No, not at all."

"Which is why I didn't want Brecken and Timmy to feel bad if I said I didn't want to teach there."

"You gave them hope."

"Is that such a bad thing?"

Raine continued working on the drink. She handed him a glass, but there was no design on the foam. Yesterday, she'd made him a heart.

"You okay?" Keaton asked.

"Sorry, I'm being touchy."

"Nervous about tomorrow?"

She nodded.

"The Boo Bash will go off without a hitch."

Raine nodded again. "Your students keep looking over here. You'd better get back to them, or they'll think I'm your hot date."

"You usually are."

"Except for tonight."

"I want to do more than chores and errands for Margot. I thought she would enjoy a paint night."

"Oh, she will. She dragged Brandt to one in December. You'll have fun too."

"Hope so, but after we're finished with—"

"The Boo Bash. I hear the name in my sleep."

"My manuscript is off, so we can spend more time together without all the—"

"Crafting and sorting and filling."

"How about a kiss for luck?" he asked.

"Luck for the Boo Bash? Sure."

Keaton pressed his mouth against hers.

Warmth. Vanilla. Delicious.

He increased the pressure of his lips on hers, and she did the same. His pulse accelerated. If only they were alone…

But they weren't.

Keaton allowed his lips to linger before backing away.

She smiled up at him, almost shyly. She hadn't ever looked at him like that.

"That should bring us plenty of luck," he said.

His cell rang. Keaton glanced at the unknown number, but he recognized the area code—Boston. "I need to take this."

"I'll bring your drink over."

Keaton stepped outside. "Hello."

"Keaton Andrews?" a female voice asked.

"Yes."

"This is Dr. Janice Gomez with the World Languages and Cultures department."

"Oh, yes, Dr. Gomez, I've read your work on Hofstaðir." The paper on the Viking settlement in Iceland had fascinated Keaton. "How are you doing?"

"I'm in a pickle."

A pickle? "Anything I can do to help?"

"You applied for a position that's supposed to start next semester. But another professor needs to take a medical leave. We're not prepared to fill the first position, but I was wondering…hoping…you would fill another position through finals this semester. We should know in November about the first position, which you're in consideration for."

His heart stilled. He forced himself to breathe. "How many classes?"

"Two. Undergraduate."

He'd done that before. "When do you need me?"

"Yesterday." Dr. Gomez's laugh sounded forced. "The thirty-first at the latest so you're ready to teach on November first."

Next Monday. "That's quick."

"I realize this makes for a sudden relocation, so I won't make you decide on the spot, but I need a decision by Thursday morning, or I'll move on to the next candidate."

"Thank you. I appreciate the time."

"Looking forward to working with you, Keaton. Good-bye."

The line disconnected.

Keaton stared at his phone. This should be a no-brainer decision. Why hadn't he said yes?

A twinge of doubt was his answer.

Not about the job. He'd researched the department. They would never offer him the position if he wasn't qualified. The university was everything he wanted. Yet something held him back.

No.

Not something.

Someone.

He glanced through the coffee shop's front window.

Raine.

Did he want to leave when things were going so well?

That was the question. One he never thought he'd be considering, yet there it was. And as soon as he finished his study session with Brecken and Timmy, Keaton knew who to ask for advice.

❧

IN MARGOT'S GUEST bedroom, Keaton set up his laptop. He had thirty minutes until they left for paint night. He clicked the link for his family's meeting room on Zoom. Mom, Dad, Flynn, and Callie were there.

Garrett entered the room and unmuted. "The gang's all here!"

Keaton stared at his family's faces. He was so lucky to have them.

Dad loosened his tie. "What's going on, Keaton?"

"I got a job in Boston. Not the one I applied for but a temporary one for this semester. But I'm still in the running for the one starting in January."

"If you're already there, wouldn't that make getting the other position easier?" Mom asked.

"No idea." But that made sense. "Both are temporary."

"When does it start?" Garrett asked.

Keaton explained what Dr. Gomez had said. "She followed up with an email, so everything is in writing."

"It sounds like everything you've ever wanted. Why haven't you accepted the job already?" Dad asked.

Flynn yawned. "This sounds like a dream position."

"It's a better university than the one in L.A., but it's in Boston." Mom rubbed the back of her neck. "That's the other side of the country."

"Lots of direct flights from Boston to Los Angeles, Mom," Garrett said.

"Lots of plusses to the position," Keaton admitted. "Even though it's temporary, it'll stop me from having a large gap on my CV."

Dad nodded. "That university will look impressive."

Keaton couldn't deny that. "It might give me a leg up on the other job too."

Callie frowned. "I thought you like being in Silver Falls."

"I do." Keaton did. "But this is Boston and a tier-one university."

"That's been your dream for a long time," Garrett said. "But what about Raine?"

Raine was the reason Keaton hadn't said yes immediately. He still felt torn over telling her he might be leaving.

"She doesn't know about the job yet. I want to wait until after the Boo Bash. I won't deny I wish the university was closer, but we both knew I wouldn't be in Silver Falls forever. But I'll be back in December, and planes fly to Washington state too."

Callie sighed, the same way she did when she was a kid. "I hoped you were here to stay."

"Same, baby sis." Garrett gave her a sympathetic smile. "But Keaton has always dreamed of a position like this."

She bit her lip. "You could have so much more than a job if you didn't leave."

Keaton didn't know what to say.

"Your brother's not you, sweetheart," Mom said.

"What would Keaton do in Silver Falls if he stayed?" Dad asked.

Callie straightened. "Summit Ridge University is in the next town."

Dad laughed. "That's a state school."

His father's snobby tone bristled. Was that how Keaton

sounded when he spoke about public universities? If so, Raine had every right to call him on it.

"Yes, Dad." Callie huffed. "Summit Ridge is a state school. But their students deserve good professors too. And some state universities have better reputations than private ones."

"No one's saying state colleges aren't any good, Callie." Mom used her don't-upset-the-patient tone. "But there are more prestigious universities out there."

"There's no reason for Keaton to lower his standards when he has a position at an elite university with kids who want to be there to learn," Dad said.

Flynn and Mom nodded.

Garrett shook his head. "Sam and Timmy attend Summit Ridge, and they want to be in college."

"Prestige isn't everything," Callie said.

"It matters in academia," Dad countered.

Keaton agreed with him. "I know you want me to stay, Callie, but there are more universities in Boston. That gives me more opportunities for a permanent position. And it's what I've always wanted."

"I thought you might have a new dream now," Callie challenged.

"My dream hasn't changed." But as Keaton said the words, he wasn't one hundred percent sure that was still true.

"You need to take the job if only to prove to yourself that you could," Flynn counseled.

"Hey." Lines creased Callie's forehead. "What happened to what you do doesn't define you?"

"We're talking about Keaton—not you, dear," Dad said.

"Fine." Callie sounded resigned. "Whatever you decide. Follow your heart. It won't lead you wrong."

"Good advice, baby sis," Flynn said. "My advice is to call first thing and accept the job. You need to follow your dreams."

And Keaton's dream was in Boston. So why didn't that make him feel happier?

Chapter Sixteen

F ROM THE EXCITED children to the smiling parents, the Boo Bash appeared to be a hit. Raine stood in the middle of First Avenue checking her clipboard. So far, so good. And right on schedule.

Her nose itched, but she ignored the urge to scratch. That would ruin the makeup she'd used to make herself into a cat. The rest of her costume consisted of a headband with ears. Her tail hadn't lasted long thanks to it getting caught in a door while setting up for the event.

The animal theme had been Timmy's idea, and the entire staff, including the two new high school kids she'd hired, had dressed in costume except for Robin, who was with her kids attending the Boo Bash.

Raine carried her clipboard and a drink. She wanted to make sure Jayden, who'd stepped up to be DJ when the one they'd hired turned up sick, didn't get thirsty. His setup was a cell phone and Bluetooth speakers, but based on the dancing pirates, princesses, and zombies, no one cared.

Raine handed a paper cup to him. "Here you go."

"Witches' Brew?" he asked.

"Nope. Rachelle said you'd need caffeine."

He laughed. "She's right. I don't see how these kids have so much energy."

"Candy, and I believe the costumes give them superpowers."

"I'll have to remember that when our little one is old enough to participate."

"Do you know if you're having a boy or a girl?"

"The ultrasound tech knows. We have the answer sealed in an envelope to go in the baby book, but we want to be surprised."

"That'll be fun."

"Tell that to my wife who keeps wondering if we made the right call."

"You have the envelope."

"True, but when I remind her of the fires started from gender-reveal parties she doesn't want to know."

"Sounds like you know each other well."

He nodded. "Our tenth anniversary is coming up. Smartest move I made was marrying that woman. She can't cook soup without burning it, but she can fix anything that breaks."

"A good thing you're a baker."

"If I wasn't, I'd have to learn to cook, or we'd starve. We don't have a traditional marriage, but this works for us." He glanced around. "I don't see the professor."

"Keaton's around somewhere."

"I've heard the two of you have been spending time together."

"We have been." She motioned to the activities happening on First Avenue. "And this is the result."

Laughter lit Jayden's eyes. "Your romantic dinner for two at the Falls Café was only about the Boo Bash?"

Raine shook her head. "This town is too interested in everyone else's business."

"It's the only entertainment since the movie theater closed. Seriously, if Keaton is anything like his brother, you're in good hands. Garrett treats Taryn like a queen, and all of us at the bakery get treated like her court. It doesn't suck."

Raine laughed. "I'm sure it doesn't."

Jayden took a sip. "Oh, this is choice. I'll be ready to do the 'Thriller' dance when that song comes up."

"Have fun." Someone called her name. "Let me know if you need anything."

She turned and looked around.

Two laughing superheroes ran in front of her chased by a mom holding their bags.

"Raine!" Margot wore a witch's hat, a black dress, and a purple fringed vest. "I'm glad I got your attention."

"Everything okay?"

"It couldn't be better." Margot's blue eyes twinkled. "You've set a high bar for future Boo Bashes."

"It's all Keaton." If he decided to change professions, he had a future in planning children's events. "He's the reason today happened."

"Well, he said it was all because of you, so how about if both of you share the credit?"

"Thank you." She and Keaton made a great team. "And

thanks for your work with the scarecrows. The kids are having so much fun stuffing them."

"Mayor Sellwood was helping with one, so it's not only the kids having fun. Tell that man of yours, I want to make you dinner once you've recovered from today."

Man of yours? Margot meant Keaton, but he wasn't Raine's man. Still, Raine liked the sound of that. She grinned. "Sounds great. You have my number."

Margot winked. "And so does Keaton."

"Go matchmake somewhere else," Raine joked.

"I will because I believe my work is done here."

Wait. What? Did Margot know something?

The woman prided herself on knowing all the gossip and secrets in Silver Falls. And Keaton was staying with her.

Before Raine could ask, Margot flitted away, disappearing into the crowds.

Raine headed to Lawson's Bakery. Kids surrounded the tables on the street outside. Garrett and Taryn supervised the cookie decorating.

"Need anything?" she asked.

"We're good." Taryn glanced at the tray of cookies. "I've got Brecken baking more, so we don't run out."

Raine smiled. "Popular activity."

"They all are." She watched the kids decorate the sugar cookies. "Not sure how you pulled it off."

"Keaton." Raine's stomach fluttered. She'd caught glimpses of him this afternoon, but he'd been making sure his activities ran smoothly so their paths hadn't crossed much. She couldn't have asked for a better partner.

For the Boo Bash.

But a part of her wished it could be for longer. One day at a time. Raine was trying. "His efforts are what made the Boo Bash a success."

Garrett grinned. "Keaton always rises to the occasion. My mom will never admit it, but he's the favorite. He's the only one who never got in trouble and did what he was told."

That didn't surprise Raine. "I can see that."

"Keaton knew what he wanted from a young age and went for it. The only thing that changed was his major. But he was passionate about Norse legends, and it was the right choice for him. Now with the temporary position in Boston, he'll be all set. Lots of elite colleges around there to give him the opportunities he can't find out west."

Raine did a double take. She couldn't have heard Garrett correctly. "Boston?"

Regret flashed in Garrett's eyes. Based on his expression, he wanted to take back his words. "I need to grab more frosting inside."

Garrett disappeared into the bakery. No doubt he'd been careless with his words, saying something he shouldn't have.

Taryn handed a child a shaker filled with orange sprinkles. Her face was a portrait of sympathy. Or was that pity?

What had Keaton said?

I'm in town through October at least.

That was only a couple days away. "Keaton's moving to Boston?"

"I'm sure he'll tell you what's going on." Taryn held a

tube of icing for a kid dressed as a firefighter. "Both of you have been busy with the Boo Bash."

Busy, yes. But they'd been seeing each other every single day. He'd had plenty of opportunity to tell her if he'd taken a job on the other side of the country.

Keaton had told his family.

What did that say about his feelings toward her? Keaton said he didn't feel like he had a home. She guessed he meant that literally not figuratively.

But they weren't in a relationship. Not really. Even if it had felt like one.

Still, her eyes stung. She blinked.

Taryn came toward her. "Raine—"

"I need to check on another activity." Raine made a bee-line for the coffee shop. She needed to catch her breath.

And not fall apart.

Okay, she had no idea when the job started. But if she'd meant anything to Keaton, wouldn't he have told her? Not have her hear the news secondhand from his brother?

It was Emmett all over again. Making plans without telling her until he was ready to leave.

She rubbed the spot over her heart, but the space felt empty as if a black void had swallowed everything in the area.

The door was propped open to make things easier for the kids.

As she entered the coffee shop, Dorothy and the scarecrow from *The Wizard of Oz* exited.

Timmy stood in front of a cauldron with steam pouring

out from black ice. He wore a unicorn costume. He'd dyed his hair pink, blue, and green to match the pastel rainbow theme. "The kids love the Witches' Brew. We should add seasonal drinks like that to the menu."

"Go for it."

His grin spread across his face. "Will do, Boss."

"I'll be in the back for a minute or two if anyone needs me." She must have her poker face down because Timmy didn't blink an eye. Thank goodness. She wouldn't even know how to explain the knife gutting her. The hurt cut that deep.

Keaton had told her he was leaving, but every second with him, especially this past week, implied a strong connection between them.

The way he'd kissed her…

Parker stood behind the counter dressed as a Teenage Mutant Turtle. It was the only costume he would find, and he said a reptile counted as an animal.

Raine hurried past him with a brief 'hey,' tossed her clipboard onto the desk in the office, ran into the bathroom, and locked the door. She took a breath and another. Tears threatened to fall, but she didn't have time for them. Raine blinked them away, staring at the ceiling.

That didn't stop her eyes from reddening.

She couldn't wash her face without ruining her cat makeup, so she fanned her eyes using a paper towel. She caught a glimpse of her reflection in the mirror.

Sad eyes.

Still a little red.

But the downtrodden expression.

The lines around her mouth and on her forehead.

The sallow skin.

She gasped.

Raine recognized the woman staring back at her. It was how she'd looked after Emmett left and then broke up with her. Twice.

She couldn't blame this time on him.

Time to pull herself together. She needed to be at the Boo Bash.

She pinched her cheeks to give them some color and peeked in the mirror. "Better."

With her clipboard in hand, she went out front. She was almost to the door when Keaton came in.

"Hey." Keaton held up an empty bag. "Pippa needs more candy."

"It's in the office." Her voice remained steady. Surprising given the way her insides trembled.

"I'll grab some." He beamed with pride. "The Boo Bash is a huge success. I hope the association uses ours for a template in the future for events. I left detailed notes in the bin for whoever runs it next year. I'll add a lessons' learned sheet to the bin before I return it to Margot."

"Sounds good."

His forehead creased. "Something wrong?"

She should wait until later, but the news was tearing her up inside. "Garrett said you got a job in Boston." The words cascaded out one after another. She couldn't stop herself.

Keaton's face fell. "I was going to tell you after we finished with the Boo Bash."

He sounded sincere, but that didn't stop her heart from hurting. "A good job?"

"Temporary, but being a visiting professor at a tier-one university will look good on my CV. They want my decision tomorrow. If I accept, I leave on Saturday."

Raine didn't think her heart could break any more. She was wrong. "Not much time."

"No."

She pushed her shoulders back, calling on every ounce of strength she had. They hadn't known each other long enough for her to become his dream, but once again, she felt as if she wasn't enough. Even if it wasn't the same situation.

Still, Raine wanted to support Keaton. "If this is your dream, you have to accept the position."

A beat passed. "It's a long way from...L.A."

"That's what planes are for."

"You're right. I'd be stupid to turn it down. It's my dream."

She had no idea what to say.

Keaton started to speak and then stopped. He held up the bag. "I'd better get the candy for Pippa."

Raine wasn't sure how she stepped out of the way when her heart had stopped beating, but she did and kept walking in a daze.

Callie ran up to her. "I've been looking for you."

"Did you know?"

"About?"

"Boston."

Callie nodded. "Did Keaton tell you?"

"Garrett."

Callie inhaled sharply. "Are you okay?"

"I'm trying to be. I want him to be happy."

"He's happy."

"Especially now that he's found his dream job in Boston." Raine couldn't keep the sarcasm from her voice.

"I meant he's happy in Silver Falls," Callie amended.

"For now, yes. But for how much longer? He's had the Boo Bash to plan."

"I'm not talking about the Boo Bash. You—"

"Once again, I'm not a big enough draw. And neither is Silver Falls."

"You don't know that."

"Does your brother seem like a small-town guy?"

"Not at first glance, but you never know." Callie's tone was so hopeful. "Besides, the position is temporary. Keaton's planning to spend Christmas here. He might decide he doesn't like Boston and prefers Silver Falls."

He was a sweet guy who'd helped Raine when she needed it most. But a dream was a dream. The chances of him changing his mind… "After my experience with Emmett, I can't believe that'll happen."

Raine didn't want to say goodbye to Keaton. Not because he helped her or kissed like a dream or tutored college kids for free. She was falling for him. Based on this afternoon's reaction, she'd fallen without even realizing it. But now that she had, Raine wanted to see where it could go.

"My brother isn't like Emmett."

Raine wanted to believe Callie, but… "Then why does it feel like goodbye?"

Chapter Seventeen

FOR TWO DAYS, the memory of the hurt on Raine's face kept Keaton awake at night. If he closed his eyes, she was there. Who was he kidding? Even when his eyes were open, her image was front and center in his mind.

His fault.

Callie had warned him.

He'd promised.

But he'd failed, and Raine was paying the price even though he'd told her he wasn't staying. He thought she understood. And she had.

Until she hadn't.

The worst part?

She hadn't asked him to change his mind and stay. And when he had to make travel arrangements and plans for living arrangements in Boston and pack, which meant he hadn't seen her since the Boo Bash, she didn't get upset. She told him she understood.

The funny thing?

He wasn't sure if he understood.

Callie and Garrett had called him out for hurting Raine. And Keaton had. A text notification sounded.

He'd given up thinking Raine would reply to any of the messages he'd sent. Still, he glanced at the screen.

Garrett: *Be ready in 10.*

Garrett: *And don't try to get out of this. You're going.*

Me: *Don't worry. I'm not canceling.*

Keaton wanted to blame his brother for telling Raine about the new job, but he should have told her himself. There'd been no reason for him to hold back. He'd used the Boo Bash to justify his actions when all he wanted was to delay the inevitable.

He closed his eyes.

Raine's face appeared—her hurt palpable.

He enjoyed spending time with her. Their kisses were scorching, but his attraction went beyond the physical. She made him laugh. Her support made him think it was only a matter of time before he sold his fantasy novel. Her gratitude for his help on the Boo Bash had made him feel like one of the gods of ancient Norway.

Keaton hadn't wanted to lose that. Nor see the disappointment on Raine's face. But he had.

In a much worse way than had he been open and honest.

A knock sounded on his door.

"It's open," he called out.

Margot peeked her head inside his room. "Brandt and Garrett are downstairs. They said you're going out."

Keaton adjusted the collar of his shirt. "To celebrate my new job in Boston."

Her face fell. "You took the position?"

He nodded. "I accepted yesterday. The job is everything I've ever wanted. It's temporary, but you've got to start somewhere."

And not take good fortune for granted the way he'd done with his last position. He could see what he'd done now.

Margot clutched the door handle. "What about Raine?"

His heart skipped a beat. Maybe two. Okay, not really, but his chest hurt. "Raine wants me to take the job."

"Because she cares about you."

"She wants me to pursue my dream. I hate to leave her in the lurch."

Margot rolled her eyes. "The Boo Bash is over. She has Timmy, Robin, and that new guy."

"You're right." The realization was bittersweet. "The new guy is named Parker. He's working full-time. There's also Amanda and Jon, high school students who work on weekends, afternoons, and evenings."

Margot's eyes no longer twinkled. "When do you leave?"

"Saturday."

Her mouth gaped. "That's tomorrow. Why aren't you with Raine tonight?"

"She had plans, and I'd made some with my brother and Brandt. I'll see her before I leave."

Margot shook her head. "You're family now, so I won't mince my words. Dreams are important. We're supposed to pursue them. But dreams can change. It happens all the time as you saw with Brandt and Garrett. I'd hate for you to walk away from something special in Silver Falls to discover Boston isn't what you thought it would be."

He raised his chin. "Won't happen."

Margot raised a brow. "You're that certain."

"If I wasn't, I would stay."

"Nothing left to say then. I hope it works out the way you want."

Him, too.

Keaton hoped Raine wasn't only saying what she thought he wanted to hear. Her being so understanding made leaving...not easier, but...

He dragged his hand through his hair.

...filled him with regret.

He cared about her. Another place and time, they could have something special. Of that, he was one hundred percent certain.

FRIDAY NIGHT, RAINE sat on the floor in Anna's living room. Milo, Anna's little dog, lay against Raine's side. She rubbed the white ball of fur. "Can you miss someone who isn't gone yet?"

Open containers of Chinese food sat on the coffee table next to five plates and wineglasses.

Anna nodded. "I got lonely when Davis worked while we were dating, and he only lived in Summit Ridge. But when I had the chance to get back together with him, I realized we wanted different things. I'd much rather be on my own, or even alone, than settle for something I don't want."

"Garrett wanted different things, too, but I was willing to give long distance a try." Taryn raised her wineglass.

"Thankfully, we didn't have to do it long. Being apart was so hard."

Callie nodded. "You both were miserable."

"And now you're not." Pippa passed out fortune cookies.

Callie opened hers and read. "Prepare for expansion. Oh, this must mean the overnight kennel will happen. Maybe sooner than we've planned."

Taryn snickered. "Sorry to burst your bubble, but I got the same one."

Pippa held up hers. "Me, too. Or is that three."

"That makes four of us." Anna took a sip of wine. "Want to see if you got the same one."

"No." Raine's fortune wouldn't change her future anytime soon. "Open mine, Anna."

"I will." Anna's eyes widened. "Yours is different. It says to expect the unexpected."

"Already happened." Raine sighed.

Her eyes stung as if she'd been dicing onions. She rubbed them, not wanting to cry again. She'd cried enough these past two days. Texts from Keaton had only made it worse, so she'd stopped replying. Unfortunately, he kept messaging her.

Raine sighed. "I can't believe I'm in the same place with Keaton as I was with Emmett. Silver Falls wasn't enough for either of them." She wasn't enough to make them want to stay. "But somehow with Keaton, I feel way worse."

"Worse how?" Taryn asked.

"With Emmett, things ran their course. We met when I moved to Silver Falls. He decided to stick around for me.

We dated for almost four years. He supported my business and helped me. It was easy. Convenient. We took each other for granted. Became comfortable. I thought I loved him, which is why I tried long-distance dating twice. But I wasn't doing that for the right reason. For us. I feared being alone again. Afraid I might not be able to handle everything on my own. Because Emmett was here when I started the coffee shop."

Pippa rubbed her chin. "He was, but you're the reason Tea Leaves and Coffee Beans is a success. Emmett supported you, but you're doing well because of you."

"Thanks." Raine had the best friends. "I was so unhappy after the breakup. I thought I'd closed the door to another relationship. I was attracted to Keaton, but I never planned on letting him in. I was trying something new the same way he was with pumpkin spice. I thought I was preparing for when I was ready to date, not realizing my heart was dating him. He was upfront about his plans the entire time. I was the one who let my feelings get carried away."

"It's a different situation than with Emmett," Taryn said.

Callie nodded. "But my brother could have handled it better."

"It sucks." Anna ate her cookie.

Callie fiddled with her fortune. "Keaton is as torn up about this as you are, Raine."

That should make Raine happy, right? Except it didn't. "He's pursuing his dream. That should make him happy."

"But he's leaving you behind to do so," Pippa said. "One of those double-edged swords."

That made sense but… "For all I know we wouldn't have lasted beyond Halloween." Raine had been trying to see this from all angles, including Keaton's. "I guess it hurts more because I'm mourning what could have been. I knew with Emmett. But Keaton and I will never have a chance to see what we could have together. He didn't set out to hurt me."

"They never do," Anna said. "But somehow they manage to."

"It's not Keaton's fault. He told me he was here to re-group and apply for jobs. My heart is the one to blame." Raine needed to defend him. "We didn't have a bad, blow-out breakup. He's off to pursue his dreams. How can I be mad at him for that?"

Taryn grabbed a wonton out from a container. "You can't."

"And that must hurt even more," Anna added.

Milo rolled onto his back, so Raine rubbed his belly.

Callie shifted positions. "Keaton's dream has always been to be a tenured professor at a top university. He's never considered anything else, which shows how much of an arrogant snob he is when it comes to academia. Losing his job rattled him and his self-confidence. You helped him get that back, Raine."

Raine held up a wineglass. "Cheers to me."

"You deserve all the cheers." Compassion filled Callie's smile. "The new university is more elite than where he was. Until he achieves the dream he's been chasing since he was a teenager or changes his mind about it like he did his major, there's no way you could compete. It's…bad timing."

Raine appreciated Callie's openness. "My timing's been off my entire life, except for opening the coffee shop. I should focus my attention there and forget about guys the way I planned."

Until Keaton and their practice date, she hadn't even wanted a romance let alone a boyfriend. Except she'd found both. A part of her believed she'd found even more.

Anna touched her shoulder. "You've got this. And you've got us."

Taryn, Pippa, and Callie nodded.

"Thanks." Raine was so lucky to have these four women in her life, but she wanted something else.

Someone else.

Keaton.

It would take time to get over that.

Over him.

SATURDAY EVENING, THE sun slipped toward the horizon. Red and orange tendrils painted the sky, the colors fitting the night before Halloween.

Keaton would have enjoyed seeing kids in their costumes again take to the street on the thirty-first, but he had to catch a red-eye flight to Logan International Airport. Goodbyes couldn't be pushed off any longer.

That meant seeing Raine. Leaving without saying good-bye would only hurt her more.

Though…did they have to say farewell?

At the bar last night, Garrett had kept talking about how

he and Taryn had dated long distance. It hadn't been easy, but that was better than not being together.

Would Raine be up for that?

That question made for a sleepless night. He didn't want to cut things off completely. Instead of a final farewell, couldn't they hit pause?

It was worth asking.

He made his way along First Avenue as if on autopilot. Muscle memory led the way to where he'd spent the most time next to Margot's. That was only because he slept there.

Keaton held the handles of a gift bag—basic craft paper—which seemed more like Raine than something sparkly and fancy. He appreciated that about her.

He stopped at the sign for Tea Leaves and Coffee Beans outside the shop.

He pulled out his phone and took a photo of it. Man, when had he become so sappy?

His life wasn't a Shakespearean tragedy. He would return to Silver Falls for Christmas. Less than two months from now.

Would Raine want to see him then? Not only as a customer...

Time to find out.

Keaton opened the door. The familiar jingle didn't loosen the imaginary band around his chest. If anything, it tightened more. The bottoms of his shoes stuck to the sidewalk. He forced himself to step inside.

The scent of fresh brewed coffee hit him like a left hook. Just coffee. Except it wasn't. He'd been in coffee shops all over the world, and something about this one was special.

A few customers sat at tables. Most stared at their phones. One read a book. He hoped that meant all would ignore him. But for all he knew, someone might be filming him. He wouldn't be surprised if a secret web series called "As Silver Falls Fall" existed.

Raine measured tea or spices. She appeared to be making a tea blend, but she never talked much about that part of her business.

Keaton took slow, measured steps toward the counter as if wanting to prolong this visit.

Who was he kidding? He might be pursuing his dream, but he didn't want to say goodbye.

Today.

Or ever.

Wait. Where had that come from?

His muscles tensed.

Knots formed on his knots. Even a gifted massage therapist would have issues loosening them.

Timmy caught Keaton's eye and motioned toward the back where the office and supplies were and took off without saying a word to Raine. He dragged one of the new high school kids with him.

Raine hadn't turned around, but Keaton got the feeling she knew he was there based on how she brushed her hands off.

Keaton didn't blame her. "Hey."

The less-than-eloquent opening wouldn't score him any points, but it was a start.

Raine turned. Her lips pressed together tightly.

His heart squeezed. Usually, she came around the corner to greet him. This time, she remained behind the counter.

Only yourself to blame.

A glance at the seating area showed people staring.

Great. Now they had an audience.

Might as well get it over with. He handed her the gift bag. "I brought you something."

"You didn't have to do that."

"I wanted to."

"Thanks."

He rubbed his palms against his pants. "Open it before you thank me."

She opened the gift bag, pushed aside the black tissue paper, and pulled out a leather journal. She opened the cover and read his inscription. "I don't know how to pronounce this."

"*Bak skyene er himmelen alltid blå.*" Keaton read the line and then he translated it for her. "Behind the clouds, the sky is always blue. It's a Norwegian proverb."

She closed the cover. "This is a thoughtful gift."

"It's a journal. You said you didn't have one."

Raine ran her fingertip along the binding. "I don't."

"Use it as a journal or a notebook or a recipe book. Whatever you want. I keep mine next to my bed so I can jot down thoughts."

"That's a good idea. I didn't get you a goodbye present."

His heart stumbled. It didn't want to believe this was the end. "I wasn't expecting anything."

The last thing he wanted was for her to feel bad. He raised his hand to cup her face, but she turned away from him.

"You gave me enough while I was here," he added.

You could have so much more if you didn't leave.

Callie's words swirled in his mind.

Keaton had to go. Dreams were meant to be pursued, not forgotten about and tucked away like a memento. "Thank you, Raine."

She stared at the journal. "I should be thanking you for helping with the Boo Bash."

This was awkward.

It shouldn't be.

And Keaton hated that it was. He dragged his fingers through his hair.

"I'll be back for Christmas." No, that wasn't enough. He took a breath. Time to lay it on the line. "I don't want this, us, to end. We could keep—"

"I can't." She held the journal in front of her like a shield. "I don't do long distance. I tried. Twice. It doesn't work."

"It didn't work for you with Emmett. We're different."

Raine shook her head. "We're more similar than I realized. Continuing to see each other will only delay the inevitable."

The certainty in her voice made him take a step back. His chest wanted to cave in on itself. "You're—"

"I'm closing the door."

He hadn't expected that. Not at all.

Keaton tried to see things from her perspective. Tried and failed. But her stiff posture and determined expression told him she wouldn't be swayed.

"I'll miss you." He leaned over the counter to kiss her goodbye.

She backed away. "I-I can't."

Raine hadn't closed the door. She'd slammed it in his face.

It—they—were over.

Hurt slashed through him. More than he thought it would. "I understand. I'm sorry."

"Don't be sorry." Her voice cracked. Resignation filled her gaze. "I'm living my dream. I would never expect you to give up yours."

He longed to reach out and caress her face one last time, but he kept his arm pressed against his side.

"That's why I didn't ask you to come with me." That was what the other guy had asked her to do. "I would never want you to give up what matters most to you."

The whites of her eyes turned red. Tears welled. "Good luck in Boston. I hope it's everything you've dreamed about."

"Thanks." He hesitated. "Can I hug you?"

Raine half smiled. She leaned forward. "Yeah."

Keaton wrapped his arms around her, and Raine did the same with him. The counter was in the way, but he didn't care. He wanted to relish every moment of her in his arms.

The scents of vanilla and coffee surrounded him. He inhaled, holding on to her because he wanted to remember the way she felt, her warmth, and her heartbeat against him.

Keaton didn't want to let go. He might never ever find this again.

Raine dropped her arms and straightened. Her face was flushed. She held the journal in front of her like a shield. "Take care."

Keaton waited for her to say *keep in touch*.

She didn't.

He didn't say it either even if that was what he wanted. He hadn't meant to hurt her, but he had. He'd hurt both of them.

When he returned to Silver Falls in December, things wouldn't be the same.

The light in Raine's eyes had dimmed. Her smile appeared to take effort. Her shoulders drooped.

His fault.

Which meant...

Time to go.

"Take care of yourself." As he walked toward the door, he used every ounce of his willpower not to glance over his shoulder at her.

He couldn't.

For her sake and for his.

Keaton opened the door. The jingle no longer sounded happy. It was more of a requiem.

Hyperbole?

Most definitely, but Keaton would miss Raine.

And so would his heart.

Chapter Eighteen

EACH DAY PASSED by slower than the last. It frustrated Raine. The calendar read the ninth of November, but it felt more like January. She had too much time to think, which was the last thing she wanted to do. Her thoughts inevitably returned to Keaton, when all she wanted to do was forget him.

November had arrived amid her tears and the fall rain. Harvest and giving thanks signs, cornucopias, straw bales, and autumn-colored gourds replaced the jack-o'-lanterns, bats, spiders, and ghost décor, but she wanted to stop time so December never arrived. That was when he returned.

She better get over him quick.

At the back counter, she prepared sachets of her newest tea blend, Autumn Blessings. Even though she hadn't been scheduled to work today, she'd come in before the shop opened to play around with a new shipment of tea leaves that arrived yesterday in hopes she'd feel better. Finding the right mix of teas and spices kept her focused. Customers would love this.

Raine spooned the new blend into a sachet. "Last one."

Her job was done, but she didn't feel as good as she

hoped.

Keep going.

She poured the remaining mix of tea leaves and spices into a jar and wrote the blend's name on it. Tomorrow, Robin could make a fancy label to replace the handwritten one.

It turned out Robin had an eye for design. She'd made the shop a new logo. The branding sheet included colors and fonts that Timmy used to overhaul the website for a class project. He'd added an online store. Raine had been meaning to do that, but she hadn't had the time. Now, Tea Leaves and Coffee Beans was completely branded. That made her happy.

She set down the items and wiped up the bits of mixture she'd spilled.

Yet, something was missing.

You're lonely.

The words echoed in Raine's head.

Callie had said it first, followed by Anna, Pippa, and finally Taryn. Even Timmy, Robin, Parker, Amanda, Jon, and their newest employee Siobhan kept asking if Raine felt okay.

Physically, Raine was fine. More staff meant more days off for her. She slept and ate three meals a day. But being at Tea Leaves and Coffee Beans was better than being at home where it was too quiet. Things weren't as chaotic at the shop, and she enjoyed the din of the customers and her staff chatting behind the counter.

She missed Keaton.

Her chest tightened as if a ton of coffee beans had been

dumped on top of her. She wanted to force the memories away, but that didn't always work.

Raine had made her choice, and it was the right one. She hadn't wanted another long-distance relationship with a man who wanted different things than her.

Been there, done that, not about to try again.

Not because she didn't care for Keaton.

She did.

Raine had realized somewhere along the way she'd fallen in love with him. That was why she missed him and why the hurt was still so raw.

But he wanted a completely different life than her.

It would never work. She wouldn't want to even try.

She'd learned that with Emmett. When she'd tried with him, and kept on trying, she only ended up being hurt more.

Keaton had his dreams, and so did she.

That was life.

Lonely or not, Raine was living her dream. Mom and Dad would have wanted this for her. She kept telling herself that. One of these times, the words had to sink in, right?

And someday, she would meet a guy who wanted the same things as her. Anna was correct. A person couldn't force a relationship, and Raine wouldn't. Lesson learned, times two.

Whatever guy was out there for her, she only hoped he didn't show up soon. She needed to get over Keaton first.

The bell on the door jingled.

Margot sashayed inside with a magazine in hand and a big grin on her face. "You won't believe it!"

Raine wiped her hands. "What?"

"Our Boo Bash Scavenger Hunt was listed as one of the top-ten Halloween events in the state of Washington." Margot opened the magazine. "Look. We're number seven."

Raine scanned the article. The photos of kids wearing their costumes, making cards for residents of senior living centers, and stuffing one of the scarecrows brought a rush of memories of Keaton.

Margot smiled. "This is fabulous. Excellent publicity for Silver Falls."

Raine forced a smile. "It is."

"You should be proud of yourself."

"I am, but I didn't put on the event alone."

"No, you didn't." Margot waved the magazine in the air. "But don't let things not working out with Keaton ruin this accomplishment. I owe you an apology for interfering and trying to matchmake when you told me you weren't interested. But this article ranks up there with the kind of press the Christmas decorating contest gets. You should be celebrating. Not moping."

Am I moping? Raine hoped not.

"It is a big deal." She tried to sound enthusiastic, but she wasn't sure if she succeeded. "I hope it brings new visitors to town for the Harvest Festival. And now that we have a new policy on events for the association, no one will be saddled with an event the way I was."

That had been decided at the October meeting. And Pippa, the organizer of the Harvest Festival, was making it easy this year. Raine only had to put a few decorations in her front window and add another autumn drink to the menu temporarily. Speaking of which…

"I created a new tea blend. Would you like a sample on the house? You'll be the second taster after me."

Margot grinned. "I'd be delighted. I'll sit at a table where I can read the article again."

Margot meant she wanted to share it with every person who entered the coffee shop. "Enjoy yourself. I'll bring over the tea when it's ready."

Once, the tea had steeped long enough Raine delivered the cup to Margot. "I didn't add sugar because I wanted your opinion on the flavors alone. You can add some after the first sip."

Margot's blue eyes twinkled. She raised the cup to her mouth and blew. "Old habit of mine after I burned my tongue once."

She took a sip. Tilted her head. Closed her eyes.

Raine held her breath.

Margot took another sip and swallowed. "Simply divine. All the best things of autumn in this cup."

A thrill shot through Raine. "That's why I named it Autumn Blessings."

"Perfect name. You're a blessing to this town, Raine Hanover." Margot took another sip. "This is my new favorite of yours. I thought of your pumpkin spice drinks as the quintessential autumn taste, but this one puts the others to shame."

Raine wiggled her toes. "Thank you."

Margot took another sip. "Do you have the sachets for

sale yet?"

"I do. I finished them before you arrived. I can bag them now."

"Perfect. I'll pay on my way out."

Raine headed behind the counter and prepared the tea for Margot.

The bell jingled.

Someone gasped.

Raine looked up to see Emmett.

He came up to the counter. "Hi, Raine."

She stared in disbelief. "What are you doing here?"

"Wanted a cup of my favorite coffee from my favorite barista."

His jeans and boots were the same, but he'd cut his hair and trimmed his beard, so it was more like scruff. He wore a maroon Henley with the sleeves pushed up on his forearms as if to show off his tattoos. "You haven't answered my calls or replied to my texts."

She waited for regret, attraction, something to hit.

Nothing did. "Been busy."

I'm over him for real.

That gave her hope she would be over Keaton soon.

Raine poured him a cup of coffee with a dash of almond milk and a splash of vanilla syrup. She handed it to him. "Here you go."

He took a sip. "My favorite. I've been to more than a dozen coffee shops, and nobody gets the ingredients right. They come close, but…thanks."

"Looking for another box?" Raine had no idea why he

was here. She'd heard he'd been home to see family over Labor Day, but he hadn't stopped by. Not seeing each other had taken effort on his part. Which was why his visit surprised her. "I'm positive you got everything out of my garage in July."

He took another sip and smiled. "I'm not looking for another box."

His smile used to make her stomach flutter. It did nothing for her now.

Emmett stared at her through his thick eyelashes.

Oh, no. She recognized that look. He'd been able to get her to try long distance twice, to store his stuff from his apartment when his mom said no, but no way would Raine go there again.

Yes, Emmett was still handsome. That bad-boy vibe was as strong as ever, but he did absolutely nothing for her.

Zero.

Welcome relief poured through her.

Raine had to be careful what she said. She wasn't alone there. Whatever she said could be heard. Her and Emmett's discussion would go viral on the Silver Falls gossip network in minutes.

As he leaned toward her, he gave her his best you-know-you-want-me look. "Raine."

One word, but the way he said her name used to make her melt into a pile of goo. Only this time, it didn't. Her ego did a happy dance, but her heart...

Wanted Keaton, not Emmett.

She took a breath. Weighed her words once more.

"There's nothing here for you."

Emmett's eyes widened. His face scrunched, and he drew back. "Are you sure?"

Raine understood the confusion in his voice. She'd never said no to him. Probably why she'd avoided his calls and texts. She'd cared for him and thought she would spend the rest of her life with him. But his actions, the way he'd flitted in and out of her life before dumping her for good, hadn't helped his cause. And he hadn't apologized for any of that, which told her he was still putting himself first.

Raine nodded.

He took a sip as if needing time to think. Then, that charming smile of his returned to his face, but once again, it didn't give her tingles or quicken her pulse.

"There used to be something here for me." He kept his voice light, almost playful as if he could convince her to change her mind the way he had in the past. "I thought there still was."

The ball was in Raine's court. She wasn't good at tennis, but all she had to do was lob it over the net. Too bad for him she was tired of playing.

Game over.

She didn't want to try again.

Nor would she apologize.

Emmett was the one who left, who kept saying he needed more than Silver Falls had to offer.

The same as Keaton.

A jagged pain sliced her heart. She raised her chin. "Not anymore."

Emmett's smile slipped from his face. His lips parted.

"All the positions are filled." Her tone was firm, not in a hurtful way, but Raine wasn't the same woman Emmett had known. "Besides I heard you're happy in Seattle."

"Yeah, about that." A contrite expression formed on his face. He shifted his weight between his feet. "Seattle isn't what I thought it would be."

"That's too bad." Raine kept her tone steady. She showed no emotion. Easy to do when she felt none. More proof she was over him.

Emmett's lower lip stuck out. "That's it? After all these years."

She wanted to remind him that he'd left her. But she didn't want to be petty. "You'll be fine."

Raine nearly laughed at his pout. How had she thought she was in love with him? That he was the one for her. He couldn't love her—or anyone—when all he thought about was himself.

"Look how quickly you moved on the last time," she reminded him. "Try Spokane. It's bigger than Silver Falls, but smaller than Seattle. And you get all four seasons like here."

Emmett stared at her. He opened his mouth, but no words came out. With his coffee cup in hand, he turned and left.

Raine held on to the counter and blew out a breath.

Timmy returned. Concern in his eyes and on his face. "Everything okay?"

It was, and she was grateful.

She smiled at him. "Everything's fine."

"And Emmett?"

"Gone." Raine still needed a minute. "I'm going to clear some tables."

As she walked to the sitting area, Margot stared at her.

Raine sighed. "Please don't start."

Margot threw her hands into the air. "Start what? I don't see anything here that needs fixing. You're where you're meant to be. Doing what you're meant to do."

Raine nodded. She was, but her life didn't feel complete. Someone was missing in her life. And she hated that.

Chapter Nineteen

ONE WEEK BEFORE Thanksgiving, Keaton sat in a rental car at a stoplight. He'd left his car at Callie's house, so he'd rented a sub-compact to get to and from Seattle, where he'd flown into. If only Silver Falls or Summit Ridge had an airport.

Cars driving through the intersection, the rain, and the windshield wipers were the only noises. He hadn't turned on the radio. His heart pounded loud enough to count as a bass line and the thoughts in his head provided the lyrics. Comments from his family made up the chorus.

A depressing tune.

One composed of his decisions that he planned—hoped—to rewrite. If only *Bragi*, the Norse god of poetry and music existed and could provide inspiration and guidance.

Keaton needed some.

Impatient for the light to turn green, he tapped his thumbs against the steering wheel. Not that anything would get him to his destination any faster.

Come on.

He'd been saying that each quarter mile he inched. This

wasn't the worst of the traffic. Backups and two fender benders had slowed him down all day.

If only he had more time…

Keaton glanced at the dashboard clock. Grimaced.

The clock was ticking, literally.

He wanted to make the most of every minute—second.

An incoming call rang on his mobile phone. Their family Zoom call had been canceled because his parents and Garrett had plans. Callie, being Callie, suggested a video chat with Keaton and Flynn. Now, two days later, Keaton wished he'd begged off.

Still, it was Callie, and he doubted the call would go long.

Keaton connected hands-free without glancing from the road. He stayed focused on the red brake lights ahead of him.

"Hey Keaton." Flynn yawned.

"You need to sleep, or you'll wind up a patient in the hospital."

"I'm fine, but it sure is light outside. Is there some weird weather anomaly happening in Boston?"

Keaton gripped the steering wheel. He wasn't where they expected him to be, but he hadn't considered the time difference between the west and east coasts. "Not that I know about."

That was the truth. Withholding information wasn't lying.

The truck ahead of him rolled forward and accelerated.

Finally.

Callie gasped. "You're not in Boston, are you?"

Flynn scoffed. "What do you mean? Where else would he be? Boston is his dream."

Keaton had thought that. He loved the university and teaching his classes there, but something had changed within him. He wasn't sure when it had happened, but hearing the words from his oldest brother clarified things.

"That's what I thought too," Keaton admitted.

"About Boston?" Callie asked.

"Everything," he admitted.

"You're living the life, bro." Pride filled Flynn's voice. "You've dreamed about teaching at a prestigious university."

True, but... Keaton adjusted his hands on the steering wheel. "Funny thing about dreams. Sometimes, they come true, and you realize what you wanted wasn't what you really needed."

"How can a dream not be what you need?" Flynn's confused tone suggested his brother was brushing his fingers through his hair. Something Keaton was guilty of too.

"It happens to everyone, Doc." Callie's tone was full of amusement.

"Not me," Flynn shot out. "I've gone after my dream and gotten exactly what I wanted. Couldn't be happier."

"Then let me add 'at some point' to my statement," Callie corrected.

"An excellent corollary." Keaton had a feeling Callie saw right through each of her brothers in ways Mom and Dad didn't. "Your turn is coming, Flynn. It happened to Garrett. And now me. Callie was always pursuing the dream of her heart, so she bypassed what happened to him and me."

"Forget this nonsense." Flynn's voice sharpened. "What are you doing right now?"

"Driving." A horn honked behind him. "Stuck in traffic."

"Where are you?" Flynn asked.

"Washington."

Callie's squee would have burst an eardrum if Keaton's phone had been against his ear.

"Wait." Flynn paused. "Washington D.C.?"

Keaton's older brother must be exhausted. He was smarter than this. "State."

"For how long?" Callie sounded either breathless or excited. Perhaps a combination of both.

"Not long." Unfortunately. "I'm taking the red-eye on Sunday night, so I'm back on Monday morning in time for my class. I had an interview at Summit Ridge University today."

"Wait. What?" Flynn asked.

"Seriously?" Callie laughed. "This is awesome."

Keaton agreed with his sister. "Yes, it is."

"I don't understand," Flynn said. "Your job in Boston—"

"Is fantastic, but it's not what I want any longer." Saying those words felt oh-so right. "I have my heart set on a different position. A permanent one. I hope I get it."

"I happen to know that position is still open and hasn't been filled." Callie sounded like she was smiling.

Her words brought instant relief.

Keaton lifted his right hand off the steering well and

pumped his fist. He hadn't been in touch with Raine per her wishes. That had been the hardest thing he'd ever done. Much harder than packing his office at his old university and leaving for the last time.

So many what-ifs had run through his mind as he made plans for this trip. The same as they did now. Keaton swallowed. "Are you sure?"

"Positive." She didn't miss a beat answering. "Some have applied, but no one has succeeded."

His stomach tightened. "Some?"

"One, who realized he should've never left, er quit. But she wouldn't consider his, um, résumé."

Flynn groaned. "What are you guys even talking about?"

The tension in Keaton's gut lessened. "Excellent. I'm heading there now."

"Wait. There are two jobs in Silver Falls? Which are you applying for?" Flynn asked.

"Both." Keaton turned onto First Avenue. A sense of homecoming washed over him. That was unexpected but welcomed. "I'm almost here."

"Bring me a pumpkin spice latte please," Callie said in a rush.

"What am I missing?" Flynn asked.

Keaton laughed. "Not as much as I've been missing."

"Not funny." Flynn must be clenching his teeth.

"Get some sleep, big brother." Callie spoke before Keaton could. "You're working way too much. Like Keaton said, you need to rest."

Flynn grumbled. "And as I said, I'm fine."

"Watch out, sis. His arrogant and grumpy side is coming out." Keaton parked the rental car in front of Tea Leaves and Coffee Beans. "I've got to go. Wish me luck."

"Good luck, but you don't need it," Callie said. "I'll explain what's going on to our clueless brother."

"Not clueless," Flynn shot back. "You two don't communicate like educated people."

Keaton laughed. "You're the one who can't keep up. That's what happens to the brain when you don't get enough rest. Take care."

He disconnected from the call, set the parking brake, and pulled the keys from the ignition.

The two keys clinked together. The key ring was the definition of boring—a silver ring. Nothing like Keaton's that was in his briefcase. Legend claimed the *trollkor* kept trolls away. Ever since he'd been carrying his, he'd seen no trolls, but a surprising amount of good luck had come his way. Could there be more to the *trollkor* than what was written about it over the centuries? Something to research in the future.

No matter what he discovered, he would continue to carry his.

And give them out as Christmas gifts this year.

Stop procrastinating.

Keaton needed to. After a day of traveling and a detour for a half day of interviews, he'd reached his destination.

His destiny?

He hoped so.

His fingers itched to reach inside his bag and pull out his

key ring.

Instead, he remained in his car.

Not procrastinating.

Planning.

The parking spot allowed him to look through the coffee shop's front window.

Missed this place.

The placard on the door read *open*, but the coffee tables were empty.

A sign?

He'd take it as one.

Raine came out of the back with a wipe and a spray bottle.

His heart stumbled.

It matched what was happening in his brain.

All he'd been doing since he met Raine Hanover was stumbling. Dumb luck had kept him from falling on his face though he might crash now.

Not if he remained in the car.

He had too much to lose by sticking with the status quo.

Keaton unbuckled his seat belt. He had to take the risk. What did he have to lose?

Everything.

His throat closed. He thought he'd lost everything in September. Now in November, he knew without a doubt. No job—nothing—was more important than...

He blew out a breath.

Raine wore an orange bandana to keep her hair out of her face. Her multiple earrings gleamed under the lights. She was…

Beautiful.

The orange reminded him of the Boo Bash. Of all the pumpkin spice drinks she'd made for him. Of all the hard work she'd put into the Boo Bash. Of all the sweet kisses they'd shared over the weeks they'd been together.

That wasn't long, but it was enough time for him to know what he wanted.

As he got out of the rental car, he grabbed the gift bag from the passenger seat and nearly laughed at how wrong he'd been about Raine Hanover.

Not his type.

Types were overrated.

Raine was as close to perfection as he would find.

She glanced around the shop, as if checking each tabletop.

He took a breath and exhaled slowly.

Here goes nothing.

Keaton opened the door, and the bell rang. He stepped inside.

She glanced over. Her mouth dropped open. The towel and spray bottle clattered against the floor. She picked them up and set them on the nearest table.

"Sorry if I startled you." His words flew out.

He wanted a do-over because of course she was surprised. Raine thought he was in Boston. He'd arrived without a text or a call. If he blew this…

Her eyes narrowed as if she didn't believe he was there.

Keaton hoped this wasn't a mistake, but he couldn't walk

away from her. He'd done that last month when they said goodbye, and it had been the wrong move. One he'd regretted ever since. "Hey."

Not the best opening. Given he might hyperventilate and blow this moment, he was doing what he could.

"Keaton?" Her voice rose at the end of his name.

Yep, surprised. The wariness in her gaze, however, made him feel not completely welcome. He deserved that.

"Back in town to visit your family?" she asked.

"I'm here for a short visit." He wanted to stay, but he had to fulfill his contract. Leaving the other university in the lurch wouldn't be good for anyone involved, especially the students in the two courses he taught.

She picked up the rag. "Enjoying Boston and your new job?"

"Yes, I am." *Here goes nothing.* He remembered what Callie had said a few minutes ago. "But I have my heart set on a more permanent position in Silver Falls."

Raine's eyes widened. "You've been there less than a month."

"It's long enough for me to know."

"But everything you want is in Boston. Shouldn't you give it more time?"

"Boston's a great city. So much history and things to do. I love the job and university, but I was wrong. Not everything I want is there."

She started to speak and then stopped herself. She tried again. "I don't understand."

"Teaching at a tier-one university is no longer my dream.

I have loftier aspirations."

"Are you sure?" The concern in her gaze matched her voice. She clenched and then flexed her fingers. "When some people give up their dreams, they regret it later."

"Not me. I'm not giving up my dream. I have a new dream. A better dream."

She studied him. "You sound certain."

"I am." He took a step toward her. "I know what matters now. I only hope I haven't burned any bridges here."

"Wait? Here here?" Her confused tone matched the questions in her eyes.

"'Here here' which, if you haven't figured out, happens to be wherever you are."

A slow smile spread across her face. Her eyes brightened, and she stood taller.

Based on Raine's reaction, he hadn't burned his bridges and still had a shot. Excitement pulsed through Keaton. He wanted to high-five someone. Later. When he saw Garrett or Brandt.

She raised her chin. "I've heard employers will overlook short stints when hiring for a desired position if the candidate comes with a solid explanation and excellent references."

"My explanation is simple." He locked on her gaze. "I had blinders on. Couldn't see what was right in front of me. I believed being a tenured professor at a tier-one university was the only way I could be happy. I was focused on reaching my career goals and keeping up with my siblings. I made decisions with my head when I should have been using my heart."

"That's a lot to unpack, but you sound certain."

"I am. I'm ready to move forward." He caught himself. "Or back. Depending on your perspective. But I'm committed to following my heart from now on."

"A big step."

"A worthwhile one." Keaton took a breath. He needed to control himself before he spewed his heart all over the place and made a big mess. "Today, I had an interview at Summit Ridge University."

Her eyes widened. "Forget big. That's a ginormous step."

He nodded. "One reason I'm here today is to lay out my plan for growth and improvement."

"Taking the analogy all the way, I see."

"That's what professors do…at least this one does."

"Go on."

"I should have never left Silver Falls or you. I'm sorry."

"But if you hadn't left, how would you know where you wanted to stay?"

His heart swelled. "You get me."

"Always did."

"I hope you always will." He handed her a present. "I brought you this."

"I've been using the journal you gave me for recipes and ideas for expanding online sales. I haven't written down my thoughts. Not something I want to look back on."

He was to blame for that. "I gave you that for your solo endeavors, so recipes are perfect." He fought his rising nerves. "This is something for us to share."

RAINE'S HEART POUNDED. She couldn't believe Keaton was here or saying all the things she'd only dreamed about hearing.

She opened the gift bag, pushed aside the tissue paper, and pulled out a leather-bound book. It coordinated with the journal he'd given her. "Another thoughtful gift."

"This one is a memory book." Keaton pointed at the ribbon bookmark. "I thought I'd start it off for us. Open to the section I marked."

Raine stuck her finger next to the ribbon to open to the correct page. She read the words written in beautiful script:

I love you, Raine. Marry me?

Love,

Keaton

Raine sucked in a breath. Attached to the end of the ribbon was a stunning engagement ring. Not a traditional diamond solitaire, but a gorgeous decorative band with a diamond and two emeralds on either side.

Her heart pounded. She glanced at him.

He was on one knee. "You haven't answered the question."

She reached toward the counter, grabbed a pen, and wrote one word below his question.

Yes!

Raine showed him the page. "I love you."

"I love you too."

His smile would have lit up the town. Who was she kidding? The state. She must be glowing herself.

"You're my new dream." He untied the ring from the ribbon and slid it onto her finger. "This engagement ring is inspired by the Norwegian Rosemaling pattern. If you'd like something different—"

She jerked her hand away and hid it behind her back. "Try to take it away from me. It's perfect."

"Like us." He stood. "We're perfect together."

"I guess opposites do attract, Professor."

"I'm thrilled mine is a master barista who can make magic with pumpkin spice."

"Oh, I can make magic with a whole lot of other things than that." She kissed him hard on the lips. "Just wait and see."

"There's one more thing I want you to see."

She placed her hand over her racing heart. "Not sure how much more I can take."

He pulled something out of his pocket. "I passed."

Passed? Raine peered closer. Her mouth dropped open. "A food handler's card?"

He nodded. "I took the test online. I got one answer wrong, but I'm certain they're mistaken, so I wrote them about it."

She laughed. "Of course you did, Professor."

"Now I can help you. I mean, help out if you want it."

Joy overflowed. "I'll always want your help. Thank you."

"No, thank you." He kissed her. "Without you, I might not have realized I was chasing the wrong dream."

"You would have figured it out."

He kissed her forehead and then rested his against hers. "I'm happy I figured it out now."

Contentment welled inside of her. She stared at the ring on her finger. "Me, too."

Epilogue

December...

AS ORGAN MUSIC played inside the church, Raine stood in the vestibule by herself, shifting her weight between her white Chucks. She'd chosen comfort over style. Not that many would notice. Her wedding gown, made from pieces of vintage wedding dresses, covered her feet.

Almost time.

She clutched the beautiful bridal bouquet of red poinsettias, roses, berries, pinecones dabbed with white paint and silver glitter, and greenery. Pippa had tied a lovely red ribbon around the stems and decorated the church ends of the pews and the altar with similar arrangements.

I'm having a Christmas wedding.

Raine couldn't believe this was happening.

But when it's right, why wait?

Keaton had said that to her. They weren't making a rash decision. But eloping was off the table thanks to Garrett and Taryn. His parents wanted a wedding, but Raine and Keaton didn't need to wait and plan a big shindig. Small and intimate would work.

As he'd logically gone through his list of reasons to marry

right away, Raine agreed with each one.

And here she was.

She peeked through a crack in the double doors.

Timmy, her man of honor, reached the altar with Autumn, the Norwegian Elkhound she and Keaton had adopted from a rescue group in Seattle. Timmy's bleached blond hair was void of color because he didn't want to clash in the photographs. He took his position on the left with the dog, who was their ring bearer.

The organist played the opening strains of Raine's bridal song.

This was really happening.

Two volunteers from the church, who were also members of the First Avenue Business Association, appeared and opened the doors fully.

Raine took a breath and entered the church.

Mr. Jones had offered to walk her down the aisle, but she politely declined. Mom and Dad weren't physically there, but they *were* with her, one on either side, as she walked toward Keaton.

Friends and his family sat in pews, but their faces blurred.

All she saw was Keaton, who looked dashing in his tuxedo and mirror-shiny shoes.

One step followed another, but she felt as if she were standing on an automatic walkway being propelled toward her future.

And her love.

Eyes gleaming, he watched her.

Garrett leaned across Flynn to whisper something to Keaton. All three men laughed, but Keaton's gaze never left hers.

Not for a second.

When she reached the altar, he held out his arm. His fingers slid between hers as if they belonged there.

They did.

This is really happening.

Raine kept telling herself that. Through the readings, the songs, and the vows.

Timmy removed the rings from the pouch tied to Autumn's special white wedding-day collar and handed them to the officiant.

As Keaton slid a Rosemaling-pattern wedding band that matched her engagement ring onto her ring finger, it hit Raine.

This is real.

She wouldn't be jolted out of a daydream by a customer. She wouldn't be woken up from the lovely dream by an alarm. She would always wear his ring on her left hand.

She and Keaton were getting married.

Joy overflowed from her heart and spread to the tips of her green—to match his eyes—toes.

His gorgeous eyes full of love and excitement met Raine's.

A wedding band slightly wider that matched hers rested in Raine's palm.

She expected to be trembling, but contentment filled her, a peace she'd never thought possible, given the nerves she'd woken with this morning, but she knew.

Not only in her gut, but deep inside of her.

In her heart.

This was exactly where she was meant to be.

Marrying Keaton was the right decision and a dream come true.

Their choice of wedding attire showed how different they were. But Keaton had shown her how their differences made them better...stronger. They complemented each other in the best possible of ways.

She slid the band onto his left ring finger.

Autumn barked.

Timmy slipped the dog a treat.

Keaton's bright smile brought a burst of tingles. It might be December, but Fourth of July fireworks exploded inside her.

The celebrant held out her hands. "By the power vested in me by the state of Washington and God, I pronounce you husband and wife. You may kiss the bride."

Raine's heart slammed against her rib cage. She glanced up at the same time Keaton lowered his mouth to hers.

His kiss was warm, possessive, all him.

He wrapped his arms around her and pulled her closer. She arched closer, deepening the kiss.

"Get a room," Flynn said under his breath.

That would happen after the reception, during their two-night mini moon at a resort not too far away. They didn't have time for an official honeymoon with the holidays and starting his new job at Summit University in January, but they had plenty of time for that later.

Keaton drew the kiss to an end and then kissed her once more. Just a peck. Raine would have preferred to keep kissing him, but their guests were watching.

He side-eyed his eldest brother and co-best man. "You're supposed to be supportive."

Flynn rolled his eyes. "I am. Supportive of the poor people in the pews having to watch the two of you slobber over each other."

The organist played the opening strains of "Ode to Joy."

"And on that note," Keaton muttered. "Ignore the arrogant surgeon, my love. He's jealous."

"Am not," Flynn shot back. "I could have a wife if I wanted one."

"You sure he's the oldest of the four?" Timmy handed over the bouquet.

Raine winked. "That's what I've been told."

Autumn panted.

Timmy shrugged. "Well, he's acting more like Brecken's youngest brother."

"They don't let him out of the O.R. much," Keaton joked.

"I heard that," Flynn said.

Garrett nudged him. "Quit while you can, Doc."

Timmy nodded, appearing amused by the Andrews brothers. "Yes, let's get going, or we'll never get to have champagne."

"And cake," Garrett said. "My lovely, talented wife created the most amazing wedding cake for you guys."

Their fingers entwined, Raine and Keaton strolled up the aisle. Smiling faces blurred once again. She only had eyes for the man next to her.

When they reached the vestibule, he hugged her. "Such a stunning bride, and now my lovely wife."

"Love you in this tux." Raine ran her fingers along his lapel. "Never thought I'd find this more attractive than a leather jacket or vest, but I do."

He placed his forehead against hers, and then she kissed him.

"Enough with the kissing." Margot clapped her hands. "You need to take photos so you can head over to the Falls Café for the reception."

"You need champagne and cake, too?" Keaton asked.

"That's a given, but there's still work to be done." Margot glanced around as if searching for something.

Raine had no idea what she meant. "What kind of work?"

"Two Andrews brothers are married and living in Silver Falls, that leaves—"

"Don't get your hopes up." Keaton appeared to be holding back laughter over Margot's matchmaking obsession. "Flynn's not leaving L.A."

Margot brushed her hand through the air. "All he needs is a good reason...like falling in love. I have two candidates in mind for Flynn."

"Did I hear my name?" Flynn followed Garrett and Timmy.

"I was just saying you're one of the few single men here

tonight." Margot didn't miss a beat. "Be sure to dance with Anna."

"No, thanks." Flynn shook his head as if to emphasize the point. "I want nothing to do with my little sister's BFF and her annoying troublemaker of a dog."

"Then ask Pippa, the florist," Margot suggested.

Flynn tilted his head as if he were considering it. "I can dance with her."

Oh, Flynn. His condescending tone made it sound like he'd be doing Pippa a favor. And Raine had no idea what he had against Anna, who was beautiful and kind, even though Milo did get into a fair amount of trouble.

Flynn, however, needed to learn some lessons from his two younger brothers unless he planned on staying single.

Wait. Raine stopped herself. She was sounding like Margot. "Come on. Let's get the pictures taken. I can't wait to see the cake Taryn made for us."

Keaton brushed his lips over hers. "I can't wait until we're alone."

Neither could Raine, but they had a reception to attend and enjoy first.

"I knew you two would be perfect together." Margot rubbed her hands together, her gaze zeroing in on Flynn, who spoke to Timmy, while Autumn wagged her tail. "Your oldest brother thinks it won't happen to him, but I'm an expert at matchmaking. I can't wait to watch the doctor fall. It'll be like a sequoia toppling."

Keaton put his arm around Raine's dress. "I'm just happy you told Callie to invite me to Silver Falls. Thank you,

Margot."

Her blue eyes twinkled. "Happily ever after is what I live for."

"We plan on living happily ever after." Raine leaned into Keaton. "And thanks for not listening to me when I asked you not to play matchmaker."

"I'm happy you're happy." Margot glanced around and then lowered her voice. "Between us, I only don't listen to people when I know they're wrong. And Flynn, he's the worst of the bunch."

Uh-oh. Raine blew out a breath. "This might get ugly."

"That's my brother's problem." Keaton brushed his lips over her hair. "We have each other. That's what counts."

She gazed into her husband's eyes. "We do have each other. And I don't plan on letting you go. You're mine, and I'm yours."

Raine kissed him, a kiss full of love, gratitude, and anticipation for the future.

Their future.

Together in Silver Falls.

The End

Want more? Check out Taryn and Garrett's story in
A Slice of Summer!

Join Tule Publishing's newsletter for more great reads and weekly deals!

If you enjoyed *A Cup of Autumn*,
you'll love the next book in the...

Silver Falls series

Book 1: *The Christmas Window*

Book 2: *A Slice of Summer*

Book 3: *A Cup of Autumn*

Book 4: *A Sprinkle of Spring*
Coming in March 2023

Available now at your favorite online retailer!

More books by Melissa McClone

Ever After series

A pair of best friends, a prince looking for a bride, and an unexpected royal match… Could they all possibly live happily ever after?

Book 1: *The Honeymoon Prize*
Book 2: *The Cinderella Princess*
Book 3: *Christmas at the Castle*

Bar V5 Ranch series

The Bar V5 Ranch of Marietta, Montana: where love is found in the most unexpected places.

Book 1: *Home for Christmas*
Book 2: *Mistletoe Magic*
Book 3: *Kiss Me, Cowboy*
Book 4: *Mistletoe Wedding*
Book 5: *A Christmas Homecoming*

Available now at your favorite online retailer!

About the Author

With a degree in mechanical engineering from Stanford University, Melissa McClone worked for a major airline where she traveled the globe and met her husband. But analyzing jet engine performance couldn't compete with her love of writing happily ever afters. She's now a USA Today Bestselling author and has also been nominated for Romance Writers of America's RITA® award. Melissa lives in the Pacific Northwest with her husband, three children, a spoiled Norwegian Elkhound, and cats who think they rule the house. They do!

Thank you for reading

A Cup of Autumn

If you enjoyed this book, you can find more from all our great authors at TulePublishing.com, or from your favorite online retailer.

TULE
PUBLISHING

Made in the USA
Middletown, DE
13 September 2024

60885750R00165